#14

JUNIOR HIGH

JUNIOR HIGH
PRIVATE EYES

JUNIOR HIGH

Junior High Jitters
Class Crush
The Day the Eighth Grade Ran the School
How Dumb Can You Get?
Eighth Grade to the Rescue
Eighth Grade Hero?
Those Crazy Class Pictures
Starring the Eighth Grade
Who's the Eighth Grade Hunk?
The Big Date
The Great Eighth Grade Switch
The Revolt of the Eighth Grade
Who's Haunting the Eighth Grade?
Junior High Private Eyes

#14

JUNIOR HIGH

JUNIOR HIGH PRIVATE EYES

Kate Kenyon

SCHOLASTIC INC.
New York Toronto London Auckland Sydney

ISBN   0-590-42028-3

Copyright © 1989 by M. L. Kennedy. All rights reserved. Published by Scholastic Inc. JUNIOR HIGH is a registered trademark of Scholastic Inc.

12 11 10 9 8 7 6 5 4 3 2 1   9/8 0 1 2 3 4/9

Printed in the U.S.A.   01

First Scholastic printing, January 1989

Chapter 1

"Why do you think they call this a kamikaze?" Jennifer Mann asked thoughtfully. She stared at the monstrous sundae she was sharing with her friends Nora Ryan and Lucy Armanson.

"Probably because you have to have a death wish to eat it," Nora answered, gesturing with her spoon in the air. "Do you know how many calories are in this thing?" She glanced at the twelve scoops of rainbow-colored ice cream smothered in three gooey sauces and did a quick tally. "The ice cream alone has got to be over a thousand calories, and the sauce probably runs another hundred calories a tablespoon. . . ."

"Pul-eeze!" Lucy Armanson objected. "What's the fun of coming to a place like Temptations if you're going to analyze the goodies?

It's not like we do this every day, you know." She grinned and delicately licked a dollop of whipped cream off the end of her spoon.

"Hah! That's easy for you to say," Nora countered. Nora, a short girl with curly brown hair, had always envied Lucy's slim, willowy figure.

Lucy shrugged, her dark eyes glowing. Lucy was a tall black girl with a bubbly personality, who knew how to put clothes together like a fashion model. "Well, I think we've earned it," she insisted. "We made it through Mr. Rochester's English exam and Mr. Robard's history test, all in one week."

"You know something, Lucy? You're absolutely right. It's been a tough week, and we deserve it!" Jen sighed happily and plunged her spoon into the rich hot fudge sauce that dribbled over the edge of the heavy glass dish.

"You see, Nora? It's two against one. So just enjoy it, and stop feeling guilty." Lucy smiled at her friend to show she was teasing. The three girls were eighth-graders at Cedar Groves Junior High and had most of their classes together. Their impromptu afternoon session at Temptations, a popular ice-cream hangout, had become the highlight of their week, a time to giggle together and make plans for the weekend.

A few moments later, Jen and Lucy were deep in conversation about one of Jen's favorite causes, animal welfare. Jen was a volunteer at the local animal shelter and spent much of her time trying to find homes for stray puppies and kittens.

"But Murphy's so cute," Jen was saying earnestly. "He's about three months old, and he's a DSH — that's a domestic short hair — and he never stops purring. . . ."

Nora watched Jen affectionately from across the table. Jennifer Mann had been her best friend since kindergarten, and the two of them were so much in tune that they could practically read each other's minds.

Nora smiled and let her mind wander. As far as Jen was concerned, every pet was as playful as Morris, as loyal as Lassie, and had a personality to rival Rin Tin Tin's.

Suddenly, Nora was startled by a very strange conversation coming from the next booth. The booths were so high, it was impossible to get a glimpse of the occupants, but the dialogue was enough to make Nora sit straight up in surprise.

"The way I see it, we need to knock out the bank teller," a gruff male voice said. "That's the only way to protect ourselves."

"Absolutely," a female voice agreed. "The last thing we need is witnesses." She punctuated this last remark with a harsh laugh, and the first speaker joined in.

Knock out the teller? Nora nearly dropped her spoon. Surely the people were joking, weren't they? She glanced at Jen and Lucy to see if they had overheard the same conversation, but Jen was right in the middle of a long description of Murphy's furry charm.

Trying to look as inconspicuous as possible, Nora leaned her head back against the tall wooden booth, hoping to pick up more of the incredible conversation. There was silence for a long moment, broken only by the sounds of ice tinkling in glass mugs, and Nora relaxed, convinced that she had imagined the whole thing.

Then the female voice spoke again, and her words sent a little shiver up Nora's spine. "Has anybody figured out what to do about the getaway car?" Her voice was like warm molasses, soft and syrupy with a definite Southern twang.

"Good point," a male voice said. "Who's got some ideas?"

He paused, and Nora reached across the table and tugged desperately at Lucy's arm. "Did you hear that?" she asked in a nervous whisper.

Both girls turned to look at her in surprise. "What?" Lucy asked, calmly spooning up a maraschino cherry.

"That!" Nora hissed, rolling her eyes wildly.

"Nora, what in the world — " Jen began, but Nora stopped her by grabbing her wrist.

"Listen," she said between gritted teeth. "There's something really odd going on at the next booth." She jerked her head in the direction of the booth behind her, raising a finger to her lips, and both girls fell silent.

A second later, a third male voice droned, "I've scouted out a few locations, and I think I've come up with the ideal spot."

"Yeah?" The first male voice was curious.

"Clip 'N' Curl, that beauty shop in the mall. It's the perfect place for us."

"He wants to go to Clip 'N' Curl," Lucy said, amused. "Doesn't he know they only cut women's hair?"

"Sshhh!" Nora ordered. "Just be quiet and keep listening."

"I think you're all forgetting something," the female suddenly blurted out. Her voice was so loud that Nora involuntarily jumped, spilling ice water in her lap. "The getaway car's going to be totally useless unless you do something about those shock absorbers."

"Getaway car?" Lucy mouthed silently, her eyes wide with surprise. She shut her mouth abruptly as a fourth voice began to speak. His voice was rich and distinctive, with an attractive French accent.

"We must overlook nothing, *n'est-ce pas?* One slip and the whole bank job is ruined, *fini.*"

"Bank job? Ohmigosh, they're really *criminals!*" Now it was Jen's turn to look horrified.

"What did I tell you?" Nora whispered, picking ice cubes out of her lap. "Jen," she said on a sudden inspiration, "can you get a look over the top of the booth?" It was risky, she knew, but it was the only way to get the information they needed.

"I'll do it, I'm taller," Lucy offered. Before either girl could react, she darted a quick look over the wooden booth. She moved so quickly, she was sure no one spotted her, but Nora noticed that she was breathing hard when she sat down.

"Three men and a woman," she said unsteadily. "All I could see was the top of their heads because of that darn Tiffany lamp."

"We should write all this down," Nora said quietly, scribbling on her napkin. "Did you get a description?"

Lucy shook her head. "Not really. I couldn't tell their ages, or their sizes, but one of them had red hair."

"That's important," Nora said tightly. "The police are going to want to know every single detail."

"I wish we had more to go on," Jen said. Her delicate face was pale with excitement, and her hazel eyes and raven hair stood out in sharp contrast to her white skin. "I wonder if I could get a better look by leaning out in the aisle."

"Be careful," Nora pleaded. Her ears pricked up as the conversation behind her resumed, and she began writing furiously. The words were muffled now, as if the group was making an effort to lower their voices. Did they suspect they were being overheard? Nora couldn't be sure.

"What are they saying?" Lucy whispered, her dark eyes solemn.

"They're talking about someone named Pierre," Nora murmured. "They said they can't do anything till he gets here."

"He must be the leader of the mob. I think they call that a kingpin," Lucy said with a little shudder.

Jen, who had dropped her napkin in the aisle and then pretended to retrieve it, scooted back into her seat. Her face was flushed with excitement and there was a triumphant note in her voice. "One of them is wearing a pair of gray and black Riveaus," she said excitedly. "He's got his foot stuck out in the aisle."

"Riveaus?" Lucy raised a questioning eyebrow. "Those are running shoes, right?"

"Not just *any* running shoes," Jen whispered. "They're the most expensive athletic shoes you can buy. They're made in Europe and they cost almost a hundred dollars a pair."

"Who says crime doesn't pay?" Lucy responded with a twinkle in her eyes.

"Be serious, you two," Nora pleaded. She leaned forward, resting her elbows on the tabletop, her brown eyes solemn. "What are we going to do?"

"What can we do?" Jen said softly. "We have to report them to the police." There were two bright pinpoints of color in her cheeks.

"But how?" Lucy looked nervously toward the next booth. "If we get up and leave now, they might suspect that we overheard everything."

"Exactly." Nora paused and looked from one girl to the other. "We have to approach this very carefully." At that moment, a waitress dropped a tray a few feet away from them and Nora had an idea. She quickly ripped a piece of paper out of her notebook, scribbled a few words, and passed the note to Jen. "Give this to the waitress the first chance you get," she told her.

"What does it say?" Lucy asked. Jen glanced at the paper and showed it to her. " 'Call police — robbers in next booth.' Do you think she'll believe it? What if she thinks it's a joke?"

"She has to believe it," Nora said grimly. "When you give her the note, Jen, be sure to tell her to read it in the kitchen."

"Right." They were silent for the next couple of minutes, as Nora leaned back, straining to hear more conversation from the booth. Unfortunately the robbers had started a long discussion about cheeseburgers, and Nora rolled her eyes in despair as they debated the merits of charcoal broiling versus pan frying.

"Are you getting all this down?" Lucy asked, noticing that Nora had stopped writing on her pad.

"They're not talking about the bank heist anymore." She had her left ear squished flat against the solid oak booth, and was talking out of the side of her mouth. "They're talking about cheeseburgers."

"That's odd."

"Not really," Jen said practically. "Even criminals have to eat. And they probably need high-energy food. All that running from the police, you know." Nora stared at her best friend and groaned.

"The note," Nora mouthed. She spotted a waitress hovering just a few feet behind Jen; it was the perfect time for her to make her move.

"Oh, sorry about that," Jen said brightly. "I completely forgot." While Nora waited, holding her breath, Jen passed the note to the waitress, and managed to whisper a few words. The waitress glanced quizzically at the piece of paper, which was folded into a tiny square the size of a postage stamp, then shrugged and headed for the kitchen.

"Thank goodness," Nora said. She leaned back against the booth, nearly limp with relief. She glanced at Jen and Lucy, proud of the way they had handled things. They had done everything they could. Any minute now the police would burst into Temptations, just like a scene out of *Miami Vice*, the robbers would be taken into custody, and she and her friends could enjoy what was left of Friday.

A sudden scraping from the booth behind her made her stomach do a somersault, and the blood begin to pound in her ears. "Uh-oh," she heard Lucy whisper, "I think they're leaving. Now what do we do?"

"Duck your heads down, and act natural," Nora said in a raspy voice. "Don't let them suspect anything." She flipped open her algebra book and pretended to be fascinated by a page of quadratic equations.

"What next?" Jen asked. She had forced a glassy smile on her face and was mouthing the words like a ventriloquist.

"Now we wait until they get to the cashier," Nora said quietly, still staring at the page of equations. "We'll have a clear view of them, and we can get a description to give the police. To be on the safe side, count to fifty, and then look up."

Jen frowned. "Count to fifty? You mean by fives, or. . . ."

"Just count to fifty!" Nora hissed. She counted silently, her heart hammering in her chest, and when she raised her head she realized she had made a terrible mistake. The robbers were gone!

"Darn!" Lucy wailed, swiveling around in her seat. "What happened? We missed them!"

Nora jumped to her feet and glanced at the empty booth, furious at her own stupidity. "They left the money on the table," she wailed. "They never even stopped at the cashier."

As if on cue, all three girls ran to the big bay window at the front of the restaurant, where they spotted a bright yellow BMW pulling away from the curb. "Can you see the license plates?" Jen asked as Nora threw open the door and stared after the disappearing car.

"No, they've already turned the corner," Nora answered, her voice heavy with disappointment. "It's all my fault," she said miserably. "I never should have let this happen."

"Don't be silly," Jen said loyally. "You did the best you could." She put her arm around her friend and steered her back inside Temptations. "Let's take another look inside. Maybe there are some clues we missed."

Ignoring the curious stares of the cashier, they hurried back to the empty booth and studied the table. "Not much to go on," Lucy said wryly.

"Maybe more than you think," Nora murmured. She pocketed a half-eaten chocolate chip cookie, and then carefully shielded Jen from the cashier's line of vision while she wrapped up a water glass and tucked it inside her jacket.

They started to return to their own booth when Lucy gave an excited yelp. "Hey, look at that. They left some kind of a foreign coin."

"Now that *is* a clue!" Nora picked up the shiny penny and felt a rush of excitement. "Canadian," she said, turning the coin over in her hand. Suddenly, she felt more encouraged. The coin, the glass, the cookie . . . maybe there would be enough to track down the robbers after all. One of the men had a French accent, she remembered, plus she had all the scraps of dialogue carefully written down on her napkin. Surely the police could take this information and fit all the pieces of the puzzle together! There wasn't a moment to waste.

She glanced up to see that Jen and Lucy were already at the cashier's station, paying the bill. She pulled on her jacket, and was hurrying down the aisle when she nearly collided with a waitress. "Excuse me," she muttered automatically, and then she started in surprise. It was the same waitress who had disappeared into the kitchen with her note just moments earlier! In all the excitement, Nora had completely forgotten about her. She was about to ask her if she'd called the police when the waitress popped her gum in her ear and handed her the tiny square paper.

"What happened to the police?" Nora demanded. "Did you do what the note said?"

The waitress looked at her as if she were crazy and began refilling a tray of pitchers with ice water. "How could I do what it said?" she asked blankly. "It's just a bunch of numbers."

With a sinking feeling, Nora smoothed out the paper, wondering why Jen had folded it so tightly. The four sides were tightly molded together, like a piece of origami, and when she finally unraveled it, she could have stamped her foot in sheer frustration. It wasn't the note she had written to the waitress, and it wasn't even in her handwriting.

She sighed and wadded the note into her pocket. No wonder the police hadn't arrived. Jen had given the waitress one of her old algebra tests!

Chapter 2

"I can't believe you did that," Nora muttered moments later, as they hurried to the police station. It was a brisk day, and the pale afternoon sun had disappeared, turning the sky a dismal shade of gray.

"I was nervous!" Jen protested. "I had the note stuck inside my algebra book, and I pulled out the wrong piece of paper by mistake."

"Let's not worry about that now," Lucy said. She glanced at her friends as they hurried up the broad stone steps of the Cedar Groves Police Station. "We all need to calm down and figure out what we're going to say once we get inside."

"I know exactly what I'm going to say." Nora had already run through a mental checklist of the bits of information she was going to present, and she thought it sounded impressive. Not only did she know what type of crime would be committed, but she knew the number of criminals, and she could reel off the color and model of the car they drove. Plus she could even tell them where the getaway car would be parked, she thought proudly. How was that for a bit of amateur detective work! There was really nothing to be nervous about, she decided, as she pushed through the heavy glass revolving doors. She idly wondered if they would be issued some sort of award for heroism. After all, they had put themselves into a dangerous situation — and she decided to work on her acceptance speech as soon as she got home. Something simple, yet appropriately humble, and naturally she would give credit to her two friends for their assistance.

The moment they stepped into the police station, Nora's knees turned to Jell-O, and her confidence evaporated. Her heart began beating a strange tattoo, and she wondered if she'd ever be able to push the words past the tennis ball that seemed to have lodged in her throat.

"Wow, this is just like *Hill Street Blues*," Lucy said, taking in the rows of battered wooden desks and ringing phones. The room was jammed with people, some waiting in line, others rushing importantly back and forth with bulging files, and everywhere there were men and women in blue. The general impression was one of utter chaos, and the three girls hesitated, wondering what to do next.

"I think we should talk to that officer over at the front desk," Jen suggested. "I bet he's the sergeant. He's the one who screens all the visitors," she added a little smugly. She was glad that all her hours of television viewing had paid off — at least she knew the right procedure to follow.

"The sergeant?" Nora sniffed. "You've got to be kidding. We've got a major story on our hands, and we need to go straight to the top."

"The top?" Jen whispered, her hazel eyes glowing with excitement.

"The chief of police," Nora said with a defiant toss of her head. "And that's exactly what I'm going to do." She remembered that a teacher had once told her that if you act confident, you'll feel confident, and she decided to give it a try. She marched over to the desk sergeant and flashed her brightest smile. "Excuse me," she said, putting as much authority in her voice as she could muster, "but we need to talk to someone immediately. Preferably the head honcho." She thought the head honcho part was a nice touch. All the television cops used street slang, and it was a clever way of alerting him that she knew the ropes.

There was a long pause while the desk sergeant filled out a legal document that looked about three feet long and was stapled together with four sets of carbons. "Yeah?" he said, without looking up. He lifted a coffee-stained paper cup to his lips, saw that it was empty, and tossed it over his shoulder into a wastebasket.

Nora watched, fascinated, wondering why her mouth suddenly felt dry. There was something about the precinct house that was making her feel like a criminal instead of a concerned citizen! "Yeah. I mean yes."

"Then take a number." He had a flat, gravelly voice and was obviously not in the mood to talk. He glanced up long enough to jerk his thumb at a little machine that dispensed numbered tickets.

"A number?" Nora said weakly. Someone jabbed her in the back, and she found herself propelled forward toward the machine. "Oh, yes, I see," she said, even though the desk sergeant was no longer listening. "A number, what will they think of next?" she muttered to no one in particular. Inwardly, she was fuming.

A number! Here she was, trying to report a major robbery, and they acted like she wanted to buy a dozen jelly donuts!

She took a deep breath and rejoined her friends. "We're in business," she said, hoping she sounded more confident than she felt.

"What have you got there?" Lucy asked suspiciously. She was eyeing Nora's little scrap of paper.

"This? Oh, this is a number. Some new procedure, I guess."

"A number?" Lucy hooted. "He gave you a *number*? What does he think this is, a bakery?"

"The desk sergeant on *Hill Street Blues* never gave anybody a number," Jen said wistfully. "He always acted really concerned about people and he used to warn them to be careful, that it's a jungle out there."

"Oh, Jen, get real," Nora snapped, annoyed. "That was a television show and this is. . . . " She paused and looked around the depressing room. ". . . real life." She didn't want to let on that she wasn't the least bit encouraged at the way the police were responding to this emergency.

"Do you mind if I look around?" Jen said. "This is so exciting, and I may never get a chance to come back," she said seriously.

"Go ahead." Nora gave her a tolerant smile. Jen was one of the sweetest, most naive persons she knew, and she was always enchanted by everything. "Lucy and I will stay here. I don't want to lose my place in line," she said, glancing at her number. Fifty-six! They'd probably be there all evening!

"Okay," Jen said happily. "If I find something interesting, I'll come and get you."

Nora nodded, wondered if she should tell Jen to be careful, and then decided she was being paranoid. After all, what could possibly happen in a police station?

A few minutes later, Jen was wandering by a glass-windowed office when she spotted a sandy-haired young man leaning against a desk in the hall.

He was good-looking, with dazzling blue eyes, and strong, even features. When he saw Jen, his whole face lit up in a friendly grin. "Need some directions?" he said helpfully.

"No, I'm just browsing." Jen found herself smiling back, and decided that there was something very appealing about him.

"You're browsing?" He started to laugh and then stopped abruptly. "I'm sorry," he apologized. "I don't mean to sound rude, but I've never met anyone who spent their time browsing in a police station. I thought browsing was for libraries, or maybe zoos. Although, come to think of it, this place is sort of like a zoo." He paused, his eyes bright with merriment, and Jen noticed that he had two dimples that magically appeared when he smiled.

"Well, it's my first time, you see," Jen said seriously. She unconsciously stood up a little straighter, glad that she had worn her very best oxford cloth blouse and pleated skirt. She wished she had taken a moment to comb her thick black hair, but from the expression in the boy's eyes, she could tell that she must look okay.

"Your first time," he repeated. His eyes were solemn as he digested this information. "You're a visitor, I suppose."

"Oh, no," Jen said coyly. "I'm here on official business." She lowered her voice to a confidential whisper. "I'm here with my friends to . . . make a statement." She noticed the sudden spark of interest in those blue eyes and was glad that she had chosen her words carefully. He was impressed, she could tell. "We have information about a robbery, and we're waiting to see the chief of police."

"A robbery? Do you mean petty larceny, simple theft, or grand theft with breaking and entering?" His voice was a lazy drawl and Jen felt instinctively drawn to him.

"What's the difference?"

"There's a big difference." He went on to describe each type of crime, and the various code numbers that the police used to identify them. Jen was tremendously impressed. He even knew the penalties for each and explained that you could reduce the original charge through plea bargaining.

"Wow," Jen said when he had finished. "You sure know a lot about it. You must watch a lot of television."

He chuckled. "Let's just say I know my way around a precinct house."

Then it dawned on her. "That's it," she said excitedly. "I've been wondering all this time who you remind me of, and it's Johnny Depp on *21 Jump Street*."

"Really?" He didn't sound as if he were flattered, but maybe he didn't know how cute Johnny Depp was, she reasoned.

"He's an undercover cop," she explained quickly. "He dresses in street clothes, and that way he can infiltrate gangs and pass as a criminal." She let her eyes skim over the boy's black turtleneck, faded jeans, and desert boots, and for the first time, she noticed the tired, strained look around his eyes. Of course, that was it. He was a real-life Johnny Depp! He'd probably just come back from an all-night stake-out and was waiting to report to his superior.

"Here you are!" Lucy Armanson's annoyed voice cut into her thoughts. "Nora and I have been looking all over for you. They want to talk to all three of us, and someone in the robbery division is waiting for us right now." She grabbed Jen's arm, and was about to steer her down the hall when Jen spoke up.

"Wait a minute," she said. "I'd like you to meet someone." She nodded to the cute, sandy-haired boy who was watching them curiously. "He's a detective," she said, lowering her voice, "but he's dressed that way because he does undercover work."

"Jen, we don't have time. . . ."

"C'mon, it will only take a second." She smiled encouragingly at the boy standing by the desk. "I'd like you to meet my good friend, Lucy Armanson, and this is — "

Unfortunately he never got the chance to reply, because at that moment a uniformed officer approached them and said curtly, "Okay, Harrison, let's go. They want you in the D.A.'s office."

"That's the district attorney's office," Jen

whispered. "I knew he was somebody important. . . ."

"I know what D.A. stands for — " Lucy began, and then broke off suddenly and gasped in shock. The officer grabbed the boy's wrist and suddenly they saw a flash of metal. He was handcuffed to the desk!

Jen felt like someone had punched all the air out of her lungs, and grabbed Lucy for support. "You're . . . you're in handcuffs," she blurted out. She knew it was an idiotic thing to say, but it was the best she could manage at the moment.

"Tell me about it," the boy said bluntly. He rubbed his wrists before the officer grabbed his elbow to steer him down the hall.

"Then you're not an undercover cop?" Jen's heart was hammering so loud she thought her chest would explode.

He laughed and suddenly the blue eyes didn't seem so friendly anymore. "Oh, yeah," he said with an exaggerated swagger, "I'm Johnny Depp."

"You wouldn't believe what just happened," Lucy muttered to Nora a few minutes later when they met her outside the robbery division.

Nora glanced at Jen's pale face and said quickly, "Tell me about it later. Captain Simpson is going to see us now." She forced a confident smile on her face as an officer escorted them into a small, cramped office. A man with steely gray eyes greeted them, his expression softening when he glanced at Jen. She was still in shock from her experience in the hall, and she was so wobbly on her feet, Lucy was afraid she might faint.

"Have a seat," he said genially, pointing to a battered vinyl sofa. "What have we got here, Raymond?"

The uniformed officer covered his mouth to suppress a giant yawn and said in a bored voice, "Information about a possible robbery." He shuffled his feet and added half-heartedly, "Do you want me to stick around and take notes?"

"Good idea," Captain Simpson said heartily. He walked around the desk and stood in front of the three girls. "Possible robbery, huh? Sounds serious."

"Oh, it is," Nora said earnestly. "A bank robbery."

"A bank robbery." He raised his eyebrows in surprise and sat on the edge of his desk. "Better get this down, Raymond. Okay," he said, turning to Lucy, "which one of you wants to start?"

"I'll go first," Nora said. She took a deep breath, opened her mouth to speak, and promptly went blank. "I . . . I . . . " she fumbled nervously.

"Just relax and take it easy," Captain Simpson told her. "Start at the beginning and take all the time you need."

"Right." Nora glanced at Lucy for moral support, and then plunged into her story. Captain Simpson watched her carefully the whole time she was talking, interrupting her once or twice with some pointed questions.

He waited until she was finished, and then turned to Lucy and Jen. "Anyone else have anything to add?"

Jen shook her head and Lucy thought for a moment.

"The shoes," she said suddenly. "Jen noticed that one of the robbers was wearing Riveaus. Those are really expensive running shoes that are — "

"I know what Riveaus are," the captain said with a grin. "I asked my wife to get me a pair for Christmas. Believe it or not, all cops don't wear white socks."

"Sorry." Lucy grinned sheepishly and wondered what would come next.

"So that's it? You've told me absolutely everything you can remember?" When all three girls nodded, he stood up, and exchanged a look with Raymond, who snapped his notebook shut. "Well, I really appreciate your coming down here with this information," he said. He gestured to Raymond, who headed for the door. "The sergeant here will show you out through the lobby. . . . "

Nora was outraged. They were being dismissed! "That's it?" she said in disbelief. "You're not going to do anything about the robbery?"

Sergeant Raymond paused with the door half-opened, while Captain Simpson searched his mind for something to say. "Look, uh . . . Nora, you haven't given us anything to go on."

"Nothing to go on!" Lucy piped up. "We've given you lots of things, the number of criminals, their accents. . . ."

"But no names, no dates, no places," he said coolly.

"No, but — "

"Without facts, our hands are tied." He motioned to Sergeant Raymond to escort them out in the hall. "But if you think of anything else, be sure to give us a ring." He shook hands with each of them politely, and ushered them out the door.

Chapter 3

"At least we gave him something to think about," Jen said to Nora later that evening. It was almost eight o'clock, and the three friends were sitting around Nora's kitchen table, planning their next move.

"I still can't believe the way Captain Simpson treated us," Lucy said, her dark eyes flashing. "He and that sidekick of his, Sergeant Raymond, acted like we were little kids."

"Or maybe teenagers with overactive imaginations," Nora said thoughtfully. The kitchen was quiet, since both her parents had gone out for the evening and her sister, Sally, was at a dance rehearsal. "I suppose our story did seem pretty incredible."

"What really burns me up is that he didn't

even want to examine the evidence, or test it for clues," Lucy said.

"I'm not sure you *can* test a chocolate chip cookie for clues," Jen murmured. "Let's face it, he's just not going to get involved. So where does that leave us?"

They were silent for a moment as Nora refilled their cups with apple-cinnamon tea and passed around a plate of gingersnaps. Suddenly she broke into a wide grin, her brown eyes dancing with excitement. "Are you two thinking what I'm thinking?"

Lucy stared at her and then nodded her head vigorously, her black hair gleaming in the soft glow of the overhead light. "Possibly." She put her cup down gingerly on the round oak table and cupped her long slender fingers under her chin. "I've been going over everything very carefully, and this is what I've come up with. We're the ones who have firsthand information about the robbery. Am I right?" She looked at Nora and Jen for confirmation.

"Right!" they said in unison.

"We're the only witnesses, the only ones who could even begin to identify the robbers, recognize their voices, or describe their car," she went on.

"Right!" they chorused.

"We're the ones who have concrete evidence in our possession."

"Right!"

"So . . ." Lucy paused, and with a gracious sweep of her hand, turned the conversation over to Jen. "What would you say is the logical next step?"

Jen looked at Lucy, her hazel eyes widening as a slow smile spilled across her face. "So . . . it's up to us. We should be the ones to solve the crime!"

"Not should be, *will* be," Nora offered.

Lucy sat back and gave a satisfied smile. "I rest my case. Shall we shake on it?"

"Done!" Jen said, as the three friends stretched their hands across the table.

"Okay, now down to logistics," Lucy began. "This is going to require a lot of organization and a lot of legwork." She smiled at Jen. "Maybe they can solve a crime in an hour on *Hill Street Blues*, but I think this is going to take us a few weeks."

"And they have a whole detective squad at their disposal," Nora pointed out, "although come to think of it, we could do the same thing."

"We've already tried the police, remember?" Lucy said wryly. "They turned us down flat."

"But I know a whole bunch of people who

won't turn us down," Nora went on. "We can ask all our friends at Cedar Groves to pitch in and try to solve the crime." She looked at Jen and Lucy, waiting for their reaction. It wasn't long in coming.

"Terrific," Lucy said. "You're a genius! Jen, what do you think?"

"I think we should call a general strategy meeting at my house for tomorrow night," she said, scraping back her chair and standing up. "We'll make it early since it's a school night."

"Need some help with the phone calls?" Lucy offered. "I could take the first half of the alphabet."

"I'll take the second," Nora suggested.

Jen pulled her raincoat over her shoulders and glanced at her watch. She wanted to get home in plenty of time to warn their house-keeper, Jeff Crawford, to stock up on goodies for the big meeting. "And I'll double-check with everyone at school tomorrow, just in case you miss somebody."

Lucy stood up, too, and looked affectionately at her two friends. In a lot of ways, Nora and Jen were complete opposites. Nora was calm and organized, Jen was more emotional and unpredictable, but they both were a hundred percent loyal, and they were always there when you needed them. Lucy threw an arm around their shoulders as they all walked to the front door. "You know something, I've got the feeling that these bank robbers don't know what they're up against."

The next day, Jen was so busy double-checking the list for the strategy meeting that she didn't see Nora and Lucy until lunchtime. She was pleased that they were holding a place for her at the big center table in the cafeteria, a table that traditionally belonged to the eighth-graders.

She plunked her tray down next to blonde, pretty, spacy Tracy Douglas, who greeted her with a squeal of delight. "I thought you'd never get here! I thought I'd die if I had to wait a minute longer!"

"What's up?" Jen asked, puzzled. She glanced at her watch and started to tackle her large vegetable salad.

"Don't play games with me. You know what's up," Tracy said, waving a finger at her playfully. "In fact, everyone knows what's up — everyone but me," she added, pretending to pout. "Nora and Lucy have invited me to this party at your house tonight, but they won't give me any more details." She paused, her face a tragic mask. "If I don't know the theme of the party, how will I know what to wear?"

"The theme?" Jen asked.

"Oh, I hope it's Hawaiian," Tracy rushed on in her wispy voice. "I've got this fabulous halter top and skirt my mom brought back from Maui last year. But if it's Fifties, that's okay, too, because I've got a poodle skirt that I'm dying to wear. I just hope it's not punk," she said, wrinkling her nose. "I don't have anything in leather." She glanced down the table at Mia Stevens, Cedar Groves' resident punker. "Unless Mia will loan me something, of course."

"Maybe she'll loan you a brain," Susan Hillard cut in nastily. Susan, a thin girl with brown hair, never missed a chance to put anyone down.

Tracy's beautiful face creased in a frown, but she brightened when Mia called out cheerfully, "Relax, Tracy. Anything I've got is yours." Mia was a friendly girl whose strange punk clothes drew curious stares both in and out of school. Today she was wearing a short black leather skirt with a heavy metal belt, a suede crop top with fake fur trim, and a pair of funny little pointy shoes that were right out of *The Wizard of Oz*. She had teased her orange hair to frightening heights, and a few of the spiky tendrils had already collapsed over her forehead.

"Tracy," Jen said between mouthfuls, "I don't want to throw you into a wardrobe crisis or anything, but there isn't any theme to tonight's . . . uh, get-together."

"A party without a theme? But that's like. . . ."

"A day without sunshine?" Susan snorted.

"It's not a party," Nora said firmly. "And I wasn't trying to be secretive when I didn't tell you any details, Tracy." She glanced around the table. "I just think we should wait until tonight to go over everything, when all the kids are there."

Susan said loudly, "I think it sounds boring."

"Well, you don't have to come, you know." Lucy's voice was curt. She hadn't been thrilled at the idea of inviting Susan, but after talking it over with Jen and Nora, she'd decided that it would be rude to exclude her.

"And you can't even give us a hint?" Denise Hendrix asked. Denise was a lovely blonde who had caused a sensation when she'd transferred to Cedar Groves from Switzerland. The daughter of a famous American cosmetics tycoon, Denise was a year older and a lot more sophisticated than the rest of her classmates.

"Afraid not. It wouldn't be fair," Nora said.

She examined the ham in her sandwich, made a face, and then carefully picked it out with her fork.

"Oh, yuck," Tracy said, watching the whole procedure with interest. "That doesn't even look like ham," she said, her china-blue eyes widening. "Ohmigosh! Remember that little pig we dissected in bio? Do you think — "

"Tracy, please!" Everyone turned and stared at Steve Crowley, who was sitting at the foot of the table. "Sorry, I didn't mean to yell," he said, looking embarrassed. "But you know I've got a weak stomach."

"That's funny," Tracy went on innocently. "So did the pig. I remember the stomach lining just shredded like tissue paper when I touched it with the probe — "

A loud groan went up from the table and Nora pretended to throttle Tracy. "You guys!" Tracy protested, "You're all so . . . squeamish."

"Can we change the subject?" Steve pleaded. Steve was a good-looking boy, with dark bristle-cut hair and a great smile, who had been friends with Nora and Jen since kindergarten. During the past few months, his friendship with Jennifer had deepened, and now the two of them were dating.

"Okay," Jen said agreeably. "What do you

want to talk about?" She grinned, wishing she had managed to grab the seat next to him, instead of being miles away at the other end of the table.

"Tonight." Steve's tone was blunt. "You know what Nora said before about it being a great opportunity and the chance of a lifetime?"

"Did you really say that?" Jen asked, raising her eyebrows.

Nora shrugged. "I had to give them a little pep talk to get them to agree to come."

Steve looked sheepish. "Well, that's what makes me nervous. The last time I went to a party that was supposed to be the chance of a lifetime, I had to sit through a demonstration of home-cleaning products."

"Oh, no," Nora laughed. "You never told us about that."

"I was embarrassed, I guess," Steve confessed. "I couldn't figure out a way to politely leave, and I ended up buying a year's supply of foamy bathroom cleaner."

"I can set your mind at ease," Jen said seriously. "This get-together tonight has nothing to do with home-cleaning products."

"It's not another letter-writing campaign for one of your save-the-goldfish groups, is it?" Susan demanded.

"No, it's not!" Nora said, coming to her friend's defense. "Look, you'll just have to take our word for it. Tonight's important, and you'll be sorry if you miss it."

"I have no intention of missing it," a voice hooted behind them. A freckle-faced boy screeched to a stop on his skateboard just inches away from Mia's chair. He had bright red hair, a devilish grin, and the kind of face that belonged on the cover of *Mad* magazine. "Seven o'clock, right?"

"Did we invite him?" Nora groaned.

"I'm afraid so," Jen whispered. "I just didn't see how we could leave him out. Besides, knowing Jason, he'd find out about it anyway."

Jason Anthony patted the fake-fur trim on Mia's sweater and she swatted him. "Get away from me, you creep!"

"Oh, sorry," Jason said, unrepentant. "I thought you had brought your pet hamster to school." He glanced around the table. "What's everybody eating? Anything good?" Jason rarely bought lunch, preferring to swipe desserts and drinks from unwary students.

"There's nothing here for you to steal, so just bug off," Susan Hillard said pointedly.

"Steal? *Moi?*" Jason asked, making a grotesque face. "Why would I want to steal when

I have everything I need right here in my trusty knapsack?" He peeled open the top of a bulging canvas bag to reveal a mountain of candy bars, apples, and bananas. "Oops, looks like I'm a bit overloaded," he said, stuffing the items back with one hand. With the other hand, he reached down and deftly lifted Susan's gelatin dessert high in the air, and then dropped it gleefully into the open knapsack.

"Hey, give that back!" she sputtered.

"You know what they say," he said, flashing an evil grin before he scooted away, "there's always room for Jell-O!"

Chapter 4

"How are we going to handle this?" Jen asked nervously that evening. She was greeting kids as they piled into her cheerful blue-and-white kitchen, showing them where to hang up their coats, and then directing them to the large family room in the basement.

"Just the way we planned," Nora said patiently. She couldn't understand why Jen was feeling so jittery. "We'll each give a brief presentation and then divide up into crews to gather evidence." She saw the worried look in Jen's expressive hazel eyes and squeezed her arm reassuringly. "Once they hear what we have to say, they're going to be as excited about all this as we are. After all, how often do you get to investigate a real crime?"

"You're right," Jen said, forcing a weak

smile. She lifted a bowl of wax fruit off the kitchen table just before Jason Anthony pocketed an apple. "But why do I feel like I have to give a book report?"

Lucy's shout from the basement suddenly interrupted them. "We're ready down here," she yelled. "Everyone present and accounted for!"

Jen and Nora reached for a tray of brownies at the same time and their eyes locked. "Show time!" Nora said with a grin.

Fifteen minutes later, Nora was relieved to see that everything was going according to plan. Jen had visibly relaxed, Lucy had given an excellent introduction, and the energy level of the group was high.

Nora was perched on the arm of a corduroy sofa in Jen's basement room, and had just finished a quick head count. It was encouraging to see that everyone had shown up, even if their motives were mixed. Probably not everyone was interested in crime-solving, she decided. It was obvious from the way Tommy Ryder was eyeing Denise and Tracy that he had come to see the girls, and she was sure that Jason Anthony had more on his mind than being a good citizen. He had immediately grabbed the best seat in the room, right next to the coffee table, and was wolfing down pizza like he hadn't eaten in months! Still, it was a good group, and she was going to need all the help she could get.

Nora saw Lucy motioning her to take her place at the card table they had set up at the far end of the room. As she walked toward Lucy, she felt a sudden twinge of stage fright.

She turned and faced the group uncertainly, her hands clasped in front of her. "Well, you all know why you're here tonight — "

"Not really!" Jason Anthony complained. "I thought we were going to see *Aliens*." Tracy pretended to smother him with a pillow, and Nora had to wait for the laughter to die down before continuing.

Then Nora quickly filled them in on what had been overheard and seen in Temptations.

"Uh, my job tonight is to show you the evidence we've collected," Nora said. She reached under the card table and pulled out a cardboard box. "Besides the descriptions of the robbers — "

"Wait a minute," Denise Hendrix interrupted. "I thought you didn't have any descriptions." Denise was sitting off to one side of the family room, a little apart from the group. She was wearing a pale yellow angora sweater and a pencil-slim black wool skirt, with soft black leather boots. She was a little overdressed for the occasion, Nora thought, but as usual, Denise looked sensational.

"Well, we know that there are three men and a woman," Nora amended. "And we know that the woman has a Southern accent, and that one of the men has red hair."

"Just like you, Jason!" Mitch Pauley hooted, and they all cracked up. Mitch was Cedar Groves' superjock, and participated in every sport the school offered. Tonight he was wearing a letter sweater over a pair of faded jeans, and he jumped to his feet to point an accusing finger at Jason Anthony. "Hey, Nora. Here's your criminal right here. What are you waiting for?"

"Nah," Tommy Ryder said. "Can you really imagine Jason masterminding a crime? Those guys have to be smart. Jason's I.Q. is probably only one step above a paperweight!"

Everyone roared and stared at Jason, who had quietly polished off an entire pepperoni pizza and was now working his way through a bowl of nachos.

"Please," Nora said, holding up her hand. "Can we get back to business?" She could see that things were sliding out of control, and Susan Hillard didn't help the situation when she started to protest in her whiny voice.

"This has got to be the stupidest evening I've ever spent," she said, scrambling to her feet. "I don't know about you, but I can think of better things to do tonight."

"Oh, sure," Tommy Ryder said, nudging Mitch Pauley. "She's probably got a date with Tom Cruise. Hey, Susan, be sure to give him my best," he said with a smirk.

"Yeah, and tell him he needs a shave," Mitch chimed in.

"Listen, you neanderthals — " Susan moved swiftly toward the boys, swinging her heavy shoulder bag, but Lucy Armanson intercepted her.

"Sit down," Lucy snapped. "This isn't getting us anywhere. Let Nora present her evidence before you make any snap decisions," she said firmly.

"Thanks," Nora muttered. She took a deep breath and held up exhibit A, the half-eaten chocolate chip cookie. "This is one of our most important pieces of evidence," she said, holding it up high so everyone could get a look.

"Oh, no!" Tracy Douglas cried. "Jason's already eaten some of it!"

"No," Nora said with a sigh. "For once, Jason didn't get to it — "

"Then it must have been nailed down," Susan Hillard said.

"But who did?" Tracy asked, widening her blue eyes in surprise. She looked very pretty in a snowy white blouse that accented her pale skin and wheat-colored hair. She was perched on the edge of the pool table, and her slim legs, clad in black velour pants, dangled in the air.

"The robbers," Lucy said, rolling her eyes. "That's why we took it from their table," she explained. "We figure it might have fingerprints."

"Or tooth prints." Mitch Pauley hooted.

"That's not such a crazy idea," Steve Crowley said over the quick laughter that sprinkled the room. "Teeth impressions are very distinctive, and they've actually made some positive identifications from bite marks." He paused and everyone fell silent. Steve's opinion was respected by all of them, and Nora silently thanked him for his vote of confidence.

"Of course, that's not the only clue we have," Nora continued. "We have exhibit B, this drinking glass, and Exhibit C, a Canadian penny."

"What good is the penny?" Mia asked. "It's probably been touched by a hundred people."

"We didn't take it for the fingerprints," Lucy

said. "But we noticed that one of the robbers had a French accent, and this is a Canadian coin, so — "

"So he might be from a French-speaking part of Canada!" Mia said triumphantly. She glanced at Andy Warwick, her boyfriend. "Isn't this fun? I feel like I'm right in the middle of a Clue game!"

Andy shrugged and brushed a microscopic piece of lint off his black leather motorcycle jacket.

"Yeah, sure," he grunted, when Mia jabbed him in the ribs. "It's really great." He leaned his head back against the couch and stared mournfully at the ceiling while his mouth dropped open in a jaw-splitting yawn.

"Andy doesn't look too happy," Jen whispered to Lucy. They were sitting side by side on folding chairs, listening to Nora's presentation.

Lucy covered her mouth with a hand and whispered, "Don't worry about it. He probably wishes he was home watching wrestling on TV."

Nora went on to give a brief description of their encounter at the police station, growing more confident by the minute. The group seemed increasingly caught up in the story, she noticed, and even Jason stopped munching popcorn long enough to ask a few questions.

Nora was pleased to see that Brad Hartley was taking notes, and whispering back and forth with Steve Crowley. She had dated Brad a few times, and had enjoyed his quick sense of humor.

"So that's the way we left things with Captain Simpson," she finished up. "He said to call him if we had any new information, so in other words. . . . "

"Ah, the old 'don't call us, we'll call you' ploy," Jason said. He raised his eyebrows and flicked an imaginary cigar in a Groucho Marx imitation. "In other words, he gave you the brush."

"You could say that," Lucy admitted. She rose to her feet and joined Nora at the card table. "I think Nora deserves a big hand for laying everything out for you," she said, clapping her hands enthusiastically.

"What is this? *The Academy Awards?*" Susan said sarcastically, cutting short the burst of applause that rocked the room. "Let's get on with it. Where do we go from here?"

"That's up to you, and everybody else here tonight," Lucy said steadily. "Are you in this with us?" She swept the cheerful basement room with her dark eyes, her gaze lighting on each one of her classmates, and resting finally on Susan.

"I'm in," Susan said slowly, "as long as you don't want us to do anything dangerous or stupid."

"Oh, they'd never do that," Jason chortled. "Catching bank robbers is safe, wholesome entertainment. You know, just like watching a Disney movie." He winked broadly. "I think you might even be able to get a Girl Scout Merit Badge for it." He paused, pretending to think. "Or is that for catching homicidal lunatics?"

"You are a homicidal lunatic," Susan muttered. "That reminds me, Lucy. There's one thing you have to promise me before I agree to participate."

"What's that?" Lucy said tiredly. She knew this would happen — Susan was being a pain before they even got started!

Susan shot Jason a venomous glance before turning her attention back to Lucy. "Don't put me on a team with Jason. I have no intention of working with this creep."

Jason tumbled backward dramatically, pulling an imaginary dagger from his chest. "Ah, I'm wounded. Cut to the quick." Then he somersaulted neatly across the rug and landed just inches from Susan's feet. "I've got news for you, sweetheart," he said in a Humphrey Bogart parody, "I *always* work alone."

On Friday evening, Nora, Jen, and Lucy gathered around Jen's kitchen table, with two other members of their "steering committee" — Steve Crowley and Tracy Douglas. The steering committee had been Brad Hartley's idea, and Nora had approved. They had simply pulled Steve and Tracy's names out of a hat. The steering committee would make assignments, give progress reports, and generally keep things running smoothly. Tracy was thrilled to have been chosen — even if accidentally — and was giddy with excitement.

"I'm going to need a whole new wardrobe," she confided to Steve, just as Jeff Crawford, the Manns' housekeeper, appeared with a homemade chocolate cake.

"Really?" Steve murmured. "And why is that?"

"To go undercover, silly," she said, tapping him playfully on the shoulder. "I can't wear the things I wear to school every day, or how would anyone know I'm in disguise?"

"Tracy, you don't *need* to be in disguise," Lucy said patiently. "I've already gone over this with you." She smiled at Jeff and helped herself to a piece of cake. "Hmmm, Jeff, you've really outdone yourself this time."

"Glad you like it," Jeff said, beaming. A lot of people thought it was odd that Jen's family had a male housekeeper, but Lucy knew what a treasure he was. A stocky, cheerful man in his early fifties, Jeff had taken over for the Manns when Jen's mother died. He was now part of the family.

"Well, I don't get it," Tracy persisted, her small mouth forming a pout. "What's the use of playing detective if you don't get to dress up?"

"Let's get started on these assignments," Lucy said, ignoring Tracy. She frowned at the sheet of paper, and ran a hand through her thick dark hair. "Nora, you're doing surveillance at Clip 'n' Curl, right?"

"Right. I'm going there tomorrow afternoon."

"That should be my assignment," Tracy objected. "I love beauty shops, and Clip 'n' Curl does the best highlighting jobs in town." She lifted a lock of her shiny blonde hair and examined it carefully. "Plus surveillance sounds like a lot of fun."

"I'm not going there to get my hair done,

Tracy," Nora explained. "I'm going to hang around watching who comes in and out. That's what surveillance is. You stand around for hours hoping you spot something."

"Oh." Tracy took a bite of cake and delicately wiped her lips. "Then you can have it," she said graciously. "It doesn't sound like fun at all."

"Thank you."

"Steve, you offered to take the drinking glass to the lab for us?" Lucy asked, consulting her notes.

"Check. There's a forensic lab over on Peyton. I'm hoping they can lift some prints off the glass." Steve looked handsome in a blue shaker knit sweater and jeans, and Nora noticed that Jen couldn't keep her eyes off him.

"I hope so, too," Jen said. "Maybe that would give us the kind of hard evidence that would impress Captain Simpson."

"Don't count on it," Steve cautioned. "The person I talked to said that she's afraid most of the prints will be smudged, but that she'll do the best she can."

"By the way, did you tell her what you wanted this for?" Lucy asked.

"Nope. You said everything had to be confidential, so I just said it was a class project. It is, in a way." He paused and looked at Lucy.

"What's your assignment? I suppose you're saving the most dangerous job for yourself?" His bright eyes were teasing.

"Not dangerous, just fattening," Lucy replied. "Jen and I are going back to Temptations to interview the waitresses. It just might be that one of them knows the robbers, or that they've been in there before."

"Sounds like a good move," Steve agreed. "Well," he said, reaching for his jacket, "I guess that does it. Good luck, everybody."

"Wait a minute!" Tracy protested. She looked around the table, her features contorted in a frown. "What about me? I don't have an assignment!"

"Oh," Lucy said, exchanging a quick look with Nora. "How could I have forgotten that?" She flipped quickly through her notes, bit her lip, and said, "Here's something for you, Tracy. I need someone to check out the bank. Are you interested?"

"Of course," Tracy said, beaming. "What am I looking for?"

"Just keep your eyes and ears open for clues. After all, it might be an inside job, so if anything looks suspicious, make a note of it." She breathed a sigh of relief. She was glad she managed to figure out something that Tracy could do without getting into trouble.

"I'll do my best," Tracy promised. "The bank — first thing tomorrow."

Nora rolled her eyes. "Tomorrow's Saturday, Tracy. The bank's closed."

"I knew that," Tracy said defensively. "First thing Monday, then. After school, I mean." She settled back in her chair and breathed a happy sigh. "Now, what kind of a budget do we have for undercover clothes?"

Chapter 5

The next morning was bright and clear, and Nora dressed quickly in a pale pink Forenza sweater and her very best jeans before hurrying down to breakfast. She had spent a frantic few minutes trying to decide what to do about her hair — after all, she was staking out a beauty salon later that morning — but had finally decided to wear it the way she always did.

The delectable smell of blueberry pancakes hit her the moment she walked into the kitchen and she noticed that her mother had already set a place for her. Saturdays were always hectic at the Ryans'. Since both her parents worked, they used the weekends as a time to catch up on household chores, and Sally and Nora were expected to pitch in.

"Are you going into the office today, Mom?" Nora asked, sliding into her seat. She was surprised to see that her mother was wearing a crisp navy suit and silk blouse, instead of her usual weekend attire of jeans and a sweatshirt.

"I've got an eleven o'clock meeting with a client," said Mrs. Ryan, wrinkling her nose. "Not the ideal way to spend a Saturday morning, but it's the only time he could make it," she said cheerfully. Jessica Ryan was an attorney with the Legal Aid Society, and was used to putting in long hours and lots of overtime for her job. "I'm afraid we'll have to juggle some of the jobs around," she said, glancing at the list posted on the fridge. "I'm down for cleaning up the kitchen, but. . . ."

"We'll do it, Mom," Nora offered. She glanced at Sally, her older sister, who pretended to be absorbed in the latest issue of *Dance* magazine. Although Sally was a freshman at a nearby college, her goal in life was to become a professional dancer. Besides being a talented ballerina, Sally was what her mother called a "selective listener," meaning she played deaf occasionally — like whenever housework was mentioned. "I said, 'we'll be glad to clean up,' won't we, Sally?" Nora said loudly, nudging her sister's elbow off the table.

"What? Clean up? Oh, yes, of course," Sally said. She blinked theatrically as if she were waking up from a dream and coolly surveyed the kitchen. Nora had to admit that it *was* quite an impressive act if you hadn't seen it before. "You do the pots and pans," she said grandly. "I have to watch my ankles, you know, and I don't want to strain them by standing at the sink," she said seriously. She was wearing black stirrup pants with raspberry-colored leg-warmers, and she stretched out one long leg and inspected it critically. "I'm afraid I may have a slight stress fracture from all those *pliés* we did in rehearsal yesterday."

"Stress fracture? Hmm," Nora said sympathetically, exchanging an amused look with her mother. "Amazing. That's the third one this month. Oh, well, that lets you off the hook as far as the pots and pans are concerned." She paused, a mischievous light creeping into her brown eyes. "I certainly wouldn't want you to get dishpan feet!"

Later, when Nora was up to her arms in sudsy water, the phone rang.

"I just wanted to see if you had left yet," Jen said, her bright voice racing over the wire.

"Well, I obviously haven't," Nora teased her. She tucked the receiver against her chin and continued to tackle the pots. "I thought I'd go to Clip 'N' Curl around eleven o'clock. There should be a lot of customers then, and I'm hoping I can just slip in without attracting a lot of attention."

"But what are you going to do there, exactly?" Jen asked curiously. "I wouldn't know where to start."

Nora thought for a moment. "I don't really have a plan in mind," she said slowly. "We know that Clip 'N' Curl must be involved in the robbery somehow if they're going to park the getaway car near there."

"Mmm, I suppose you're right. But we don't know if they picked it for the location, or because somebody in the ring works there."

"I know," Nora admitted. "That's a real problem, too. I think someone who works there must be involved, because the location doesn't make sense. It's not even near the bank."

"Unless they didn't want to park a getaway car near the bank, because it would look too suspicious." Jen paused, thinking. "I don't know, there are just so many unanswered questions about this whole thing. Nora, have you thought about asking your mother for advice? She must know a lot more about robberies than we do."

Nora laughed and nearly dropped a heavy cast-iron skillet she was washing. "Ask my mother? You've got to be kidding. She's a lawyer, not a detective. She can't even figure out the plots on *Murder, She Wrote*."

"Oh." Another pause. "Well, would you like me to come with you to Clip 'N' Curl?" Jennifer offered. "Two heads are better than one, and all that."

"Not in a beauty salon, I'm afraid. It's going to be tough enough for me to prowl around there without making a fool out of myself. No, I think I better do this one alone. We can get together afterward, if you like."

"Lunch at Luigi's," Jen said promptly. "I'll call Lucy."

"Done!"

An hour later, Nora hesitated outside the Clip 'N' Curl. It was one of Cedar Groves' most exclusive styling salons, and no effort had been spared to disguise the fact that the classy-looking establishment was actually a "beauty shop." Silk-curtained French windows discreetly shielded the patrons from curious passersby, and two potted trees guarded the entrance. It could be anything from an expensive private club to a high-priced boutique,

Nora thought, scanning the façade. It didn't look the least little bit like a place that would be involved in a bank robbery.

If only she knew what she should be looking for! She and Lucy had agreed that her assignment was just to get a feel for the place, but she wished she was going after something more specific. The only direct link she could think of — besides the getaway car — was the woman with the Southern accent. Maybe she worked here, Nora thought, or had her hair done here.

Realizing she wasn't getting anywhere standing outside, she took a deep breath and pushed open the stylish bleached oak door. She was surprised to find herself in a large circular room with soft lighting and deep pile carpeting. The room was boldly decorated in black and white, and classical music played dimly somewhere in the background. A blonde woman sat at a long curvy desk that seemed to be topped with black marble, and when she saw Nora she put aside a magazine and flashed a brittle smile.

"Yes?" she said. "May I help you?"

Nora was stumped, and wished she had prepared herself a little better. She had assumed that Clip 'N' Curl would be like the other beauty shops she had been to — noisy, crowded, bustling with activity — and that she could blend in easily. It was obvious from the way the woman was looking at her jeans and sneakers that she stood out like a catfish in an aquarium.

Nora smiled, pretending to be absorbed in a French Impressionist print on the far wall, while her mind searched desperately for something to say. After a moment, when the woman's eyes were boring holes in her back, she turned and said hesitantly, "I . . . uh, need to do something with my hair, but I haven't quite yet decided what." That was probably a safe thing to say, she decided, and it didn't commit her to anything.

The blonde woman didn't seem surprised by her revelation, and said simply, "A lot of our customers find themselves in that predicament. Would you like a consultation with Monsieur André?"

"A consultation?" Nora repeated. "Yes, I think that would be nice."

"Please have a seat."

The woman talked softly into an intercom while Nora settled into an uncomfortable high-tech white leather chair. She would have liked to flip through a magazine or two, but nothing was available. She couldn't get over Clip 'N'

Curl. It was absolutely unlike every other beauty shop she had ever been to — not a curling iron or roller in sight. And more amazingly, there wasn't even a cash register on the desk.

She was wondering where the blonde woman put the cash when a thin, nervous-looking young man appeared before her.

"Mademoiselle would like a consultation," he said in a soft voice.

"I . . . yes, I would," Nora said, standing up. He was only a couple of inches taller than she was and he was wearing a white lab coat like a doctor in a television commercial. "Are you Monsieur André?"

His black eyes nearly rolled back in his head in amazement. "Me? Monsieur André? Of course not!" He looked at her as if she had mistaken him for King Tut and motioned for her to follow him. "I am Georges. I will take you to Monsieur André."

"Wonderful," Nora muttered, as he pushed open a double set of brass doors that apparently led to Clip 'N' Curl's inner sanctum. Georges walked quickly down a long narrow hallway, and Nora scampered behind him, surprised at the double line of curtained cubicles. It reminded her a little of a carnival fun house.

She heard softly muted conversations coming from behind several of the doors, and she decided that if she was going to get any information out of Georges, she'd have to take the initiative. "So tell me," she said loudly, "where are all the customers?"

"They are all in private consultation rooms," he said, deliberately pitching his voice lower than hers.

"Private, huh? You mean nobody gets to see how anybody else's hair turns out?" Nora joked. "Gee, I always thought that was half the fun of going to the beauty shop."

Georges gave a shudder at Nora's suggestion and said heatedly, "Certainly not! Our customers value their privacy." He walked briskly ahead of her until they reached the end of the hallway. He pushed open another set of doors and ushered her into a small octagonal room done all in soft pink. Nora could feel the lipstick-colored walls closing in on her — it was like being trapped inside a giant box of pink tissues.

"Monsieur André will join you shortly," Georges said in a hushed tone. He closed the door quietly behind him, leaving Nora alone with her thoughts.

She glanced at herself in the mirror and was amazed to see that her skin looked flushed. She pondered this for a moment, puzzled, and then spotted the ornate chandelier swinging above her head. Of course, it had soft pink light bulbs!

"Aha!" A heavily accented voice made her jump. "What have we here?" A portly man with a mustache swept into the room followed by a trim woman with red hair.

"Monsieur André?" Nora said hesitantly. After her experience with Georges, she wasn't taking any chances.

"At your service, Mademoiselle," the man said, giving a low bow. "And this is Mademoiselle Bernice, my top stylist. What can we do for you today?" His eyes were black and strangely penetrating, like a hypnotist's. Nora's hands felt clammy as she gripped the arm of the chair.

"I'm here for a consultation," she said in a faltering voice.

He lifted up a handful of her chestnut curls and fanned them gently through his fingers, the corners of his mouth turned down mournfully. Then he gave a depressing analysis to the redhead who stood by respectfully with a clipboard. "Limp hair, no body, no highlights, no shine, tendency to split ends, and definite frizzing."

"Is that all?" Nora couldn't resist asking.

"Not only is the hair in terrible condition, but the style is wrong for you, hopeless, how do you say, *abominable!*" Even though he pronounced the last word with a thick French accent, Nora understood perfectly well what he meant.

"You have the same word in English, no?" he said to Mademoiselle Bernice.

"We sure do," the redhead piped up in a Texas twang. "Abominable. And it means the same thing, too," she added helpfully.

"That's certainly good to know." They seemed to miss the wry tone in Nora's voice. She listened as the two of them discussed her hair at great length, their bizarre accents rising and falling in the crazy pink room.

And then it dawned on her. She had come to Clip 'N' Curl looking for clues, and through some incredible burst of luck, she'd already turned up a Frenchman, and a girl with a Southern accent. She felt her heart leap in her throat as her hands gripped the arms of the chair so hard her knuckles turned white.

It looked like she had hit the jackpot. And then a new thought gripped her, and it was so exciting, she almost gasped out loud.

Mademoiselle Bernice had more than a Southern accent. She had flaming red hair!

Chapter 6

The big problem, Nora decided a moment later, was that she didn't know what to do with this information! Could Clip 'n' Curl be the key to the whole bank robbery scheme? It certainly seemed that way, if the Frenchman and the redhead were working here together. Surely that had to be more than mere coincidence. She decided to do whatever it took to prolong her visit at the salon. She needed a chance to find out as much as she could about Monsieur André, and to pump Mademoiselle Bernice for information, if she could. Another possibility was the long row of forbidden cubicles down the hall. If she was careful — and very lucky — she might be able to peek inside them and talk to some of the customers who "valued their privacy."

She yanked her thoughts back to the present when she realized that Monsieur André had stopped talking and was regarding her solemnly. Her eyes met his in the mirror, and she tried to look suitably impressed. It was obvious that something important was about to happen.

"I have finished my analysis," Monsieur André said in pompous tones, "and now I will make my recommendation." Nora waited with a look of breathless interest on her face, while Mademoiselle Bernice stood by with her clipboard.

"A permanent!" Monsieur said happily.

A permanent! Nora's jaw dropped open and she gaped at him in amazement. What was wrong with Monsieur André? Couldn't he see she had her own mop of curls — all natural?

"But I don't need a permanent. I already have curly hair." She pulled a chestnut strand straight out from her head and let it spring back in a tight coil. "See?"

"Monsieur André sees all," he said with heavy patience. He closed his eyes as if the strain of explaining his genius was too much for him, and waved for Mademoiselle Bernice to continue.

"Well, you see, honey, we do a lot of permanents on girls with curly hair, just like yours." Her voice was cheerful, and Nora suddenly felt depressed at the thought of her going to jail for bank robbery. Maybe when all this was over, Nora could ask for leniency for Mademoiselle Bernice — that is, if she didn't mess up her hair too badly this morning.

"You mean it's better to have curly hair from a permanent than . . . to be born with it?"

"Oh, absolutely!" She shook her head up and down vigorously. "With these new permanents, the curls have a built-in memory, so the style always comes back."

Nora tuned out the rest of the explanation, while Mademoiselle Bernice helped her into a pale pink smock, and ushered her into one of the curtained cubicles she had seen earlier. Unfortunately, her worst fears were coming true. She was going to get a permanent, and there was nothing she could do about it!

"Have you been working here long?" Nora asked twenty minutes later. She tried not to gasp at the harsh chemical fumes that were wafting up from her hair.

"No, I just started," Mademoiselle Bernice said, nearly gassing Nora with another heady dose of something she called "developer."

Nora waited for her to say more, but she seemed absorbed in a country song on the radio, nodding her head and mouthing the words as she worked. "Do you like Willie Nelson?" Nora asked, on a sudden inspiration.

"I just love him to death!" the redhead replied. "Makes me homesick, though." She gave a wistful smile. "I can't hear any of his songs without thinking of Texas."

"Oh, you're from Texas? That's nice." Nora smiled politely, tucking away the bit of information. Texas, Texas, she thought, her mind struggling to make a connection. Texas had nothing to do with bank robberies, did it? Unless you counted Jesse James, and that seemed a little farfetched. . . . "Pardon me for asking, but Monsieur André calls you Mademoiselle Bernice, so I wondered if you could be French." Nora couldn't believe she managed to keep a straight face through that incredible speech, but the red-haired girl didn't seem to think the question was odd.

"Oh, a lot of people think that," she said amazingly. She glanced over her shoulder and lowered her voice to a husky whisper. "But I'll let you in on a little secret, I'm not French at all."

"No! Really?"

"Really." She nodded, her blue eyes serious. "Monsieur André just calls me that because he thinks it gives the place a little class."

"Ah. That's very interesting."

"You can call me Bernie, if you like."

"Okay." Nora was just figuring out what to ask next, when Bernie handed her a magazine, and set a small pink plastic timer next to her.

"You're all set for the next thirty minutes, but if you need anything, you just use this buzzer, and I'll come running," Bernie said, dropping a small red plastic device in Nora's lap and leaving.

The moment Nora heard the curtains close, she jumped to her feet, considering her next move. Feeling silly in the pink smock, she clutched the edges tightly together and peeked out into the hall. She could hear voices drifting out of the other cubicles, but the hallway was empty, and she knew that this was the time to make her move. Her eyes were drawn to the pink octagonal room at the end of the hall — the consultation room where she had met Monsieur André. Of course! That must be the nerve center of the whole operation. Before she could lose her courage, she darted silently down the carpeted hall.

By some incredible stroke of luck, the pink door at the end of the hallway was slightly ajar, and Nora crouched outside, listening. A moment later, a familiar voice drifted out — Monsieur André was arguing with someone on the phone. By flattening herself against the half-opened door, Nora could just manage to see the back of his head over the top of the chair as he barked into the receiver.

"I told you Thursday isn't good enough!" he thundered. She noticed his French accent had disappeared and he mumbled his words like Sylvester Stallone. "We need the delivery Wednesday afternoon at the latest, and it better be before three. No excuses." He gave a harsh laugh. "And remember, this is a cash business."

Nora froze as the implication of his words sunk in. *Before three* . . . Of course, the banks closed at three! So they were planning the heist while the customers were still inside. But what could the delivery be? Maybe a gun or a weapon they needed to pull off the crime, she thought with a little shudder. And bank robbery certainly was a cash business, she thought. Everything fit, didn't it?

Nora hesitated, wondering if she had enough information to go back to Captain Simpson. Then she remembered the amused look he had exchanged with Sergeant Raymond. The two of them were convinced that they were dealing with a bunch of silly teenagers who watched too much television. It would take more than a phone conversation to get them to take her seriously. No, she decided, I need more proof.

A scraping noise from the octagonal room made her jump in surprise — Monsieur André had pushed back his chair and was heading straight for the door. In another second, he'd see her, and the game would be up. Her heart was thudding in her chest as she glanced desperately down the hall. She'd never make it back to her cubicle in time!

The door was opening as Nora quickly dropped to her hands and knees, inspecting the thick shag carpet. Out of the corner of her eye, she saw a pair of men's black shoes approaching, and heard a muffled curse as Monsieur André almost tripped over her.

"What in the — what are you doing there? Why aren't you in your cubicle?" he demanded angrily, forgetting to put on his accent.

"Oh, Monsieur," Nora said sweetly, "I didn't mean to get in your way. I'm just looking for my contact. I dropped it on the rug a few minutes ago."

"Your contact?"

"My contact lens," she added in a syrupy voice. "It's a little round circle, and you do this." She pointed to her eye, and did a passable imitation of someone inspecting their fingertip and then sticking it straight into their eyeball. "I don't know how you say it in French." And I bet you don't either, she thought, watching as he tugged thoughtfully at his mustache.

"Well, you can't block the hall like this," he said irritably. Reluctantly, he dropped to his knees to help her, and for the next few moments, they worked side by side, combing their hands through the thick tufts of pink wool carpeting. Nora was shaking inside, and she couldn't stop thinking that she was just inches away from a dangerous criminal. He seemed to be looking at her suspiciously, but she couldn't be sure.

A loud buzzer sounded just then, and Bernie appeared at the other end of the hall, looking at them in astonishment. "Hey, your time's up," she called to Nora. "I was just coming to get you."

"Fine," Nora said, scrambling to her feet. Her hands were trembling, and she was so nervous she knew she'd give herself away if she had to hang around the man for another second.

"But what about your contact?" Monseiur André's accent was firmly back in place, she noticed. A nice touch. Score one for the pseudo-Frenchman, she thought.

"Oh, that," Nora said, shrugging prettily. She lifted her finger to her eyelashes and fluttered them a little. "It was in my eye all the time. Silly me!"

Half an hour later, she and Bernie were staring silently into the mirror. The curlers had been removed, one by one, and now it was time to brush out the hair and assess the damage. Nora had been waiting in an agony of suspense for this moment.

"Well, here goes nothing," Bernie said cheerfully. Not the most tactful thing to say, Nora thought, as the redhead started yanking what looked like a metal dog brush through her hair. After a moment, it was obvious that some basic law of physics was at work here. An irresistible force (the hairbrush) was meeting an immovable object (Nora's hair) and something had to give. In this case, it was Nora's scalp.

"Ouch!" Nora didn't bother to stifle her yelp of pain. She felt as if her hair was literally being pulled out of her head, strand by strand.

"Sorry," Bernie murmured apologetically. "The curls seem a little . . . tight."

Tight! That had to be the understatement of

the year. Nora glanced at her hair and wanted to cry out in despair. Her shiny chestnut curls had been transformed into a dense mat that had the look and feel of a Brillo pad.

"I think it's hopeless," Nora moaned.

"Oh, now don't you worry, we'll fix it up," said Bernie the Optimist. "A little brushing, a little spray, and you'll be right as rain."

"Do you think so?" Nora wanted desperately to believe Bernie, but it was hard to deny the evidence of her own eyes.

"I sure do!" Bernie said, swaying to a Waylon Jennings tune. "I'll tell you what, honey," she said in her cheerful Texas twang, "I've seen plenty worse!"

"Wonderful," Nora muttered. "Just wonderful."

Chapter 7

Luigi's was crowded when Nora hurried inside half an hour later, and it took her a few minutes to spot Lucy and Jen, who had managed to snare one of the corner booths in the back of the room.

She noticed that both girls had dressed up for the occasion, Lucy in gray wool slacks with a plum-colored sweater, and Jen in a preppy watch plaid kilt topped by a frilly white blouse. They had been giggling across the table about something, but stopped and looked at her uncertainly as she approached the booth. No wonder! Nora thought. She knew she looked like a total geek. She was wearing black oversized glasses, and had wrapped her ruined hair in a pink chiffon scarf. She had already decided that as soon as she ate lunch, she'd give a quick report on Clip 'N' Curl, and then hide in her room for the next six months!

Jen did a double take, and then recovered. "Hi, Nora," she said a little too brightly. "We were starving so we went ahead and ordered a pizza. I hope green pepper and mushroom with extra cheese is okay." She exchanged a puzzled look with Lucy. What in the world was wrong with Nora? she wondered. The cheap plastic sunglasses were bad enough — but why was she wearing that silly pink scarf on her head?

Lucy was wondering the same thing. "Jen was all set to order the Vegetarian Delight, but I finally convinced her that tofu and garlic don't mix. And I got you a side order of rigatoni." Her brown eyes were thoughtful — one look at Nora's downcast expression told her something had gone terribly wrong.

"That sounds good," Nora said wearily. "You know me — I like anything as long as it doesn't have anchovies in it." She dropped gratefully onto the red leather seat, and took a quick look around, debating whether or not to remove the scarf she had bought at Clip 'N' Curl. The scarf was hideous, but at least it completely covered her hair, which was even more hideous, she thought wryly. She saw Lucy's questioning look, and was just about to explain, when Jen spoke up.

"Uh-oh," Jen said, her hazel eyes serious. "I think I just figured out what happened. They did something to your hair, didn't they?" She stared in disbelief at the kinky curls that had crept out of the scarf onto Nora's forehead.

"You guessed it," Nora said tonelessly. She glanced around the restaurant again, hoping she wouldn't see anyone she knew. "You'll never believe what they did — they gave me a permanent!"

"A permanent!" Lucy's dark eyebrows arched in surprise. "But you've got naturally curly hair."

"Exactly."

No one said anything for a moment, and then Jen asked gently, "How bad is it?"

"You have to see it to believe it," Nora said grimly.

"That bad?"

Nora gave a mirthless laugh. "Let's just say it's a good thing you're both sitting down."

Her fingers crept toward the pink chiffon knot that was tied firmly under her chin, when a familiar voice made her cringe. "Hi, guys! Hope I'm not late." It was Tracy Douglas, looking terrific in khaki safari pants with a leopard print top. "Isn't it great we could all get together today?"

Nora groaned inwardly. Who had invited Tracy — and why? She couldn't take her eyes off Tracy's gleaming blonde hair. It tumbled half way down her back, sparkling like gold in the afternoon sunlight. It was long, silky, and best of all, *straight*.

Meanwhile, Lucy had seen the stricken look on Nora's face, and decided to explain about the fourth member of the group. "Uh, Tracy called and said she'd like to join us for lunch and give us a progress report." She kept her voice carefully cheerful. "Isn't that nice?"

"Very nice," Nora said without an ounce of enthusiasm. She knew it wasn't Tracy's fault that she was born with fantastic, shimmering, wheat-colored hair, but the timing couldn't have been worse! "But what could you possibly have to report?" she asked, turning to Tracy. "The bank isn't even open until Monday."

"I know that," Tracy said, looking hurt. "But I did some preliminary research." She whipped out a small spiral notebook and began reading. "Here's what I've got so far. I called the bank and found out the hours they're open — " She broke off suddenly, staring at Nora's glasses and scarf. "Hey, what's going on?" she said petulantly. "I thought there wasn't any budget for undercover clothes."

"There isn't," Lucy said with a sigh. "Nora isn't working undercover, if that's what you're getting at."

"Then why is she wearing a disguise?"

"It's not a disguise," Nora hissed. She leaned close to Tracy, her brown eyes flashing. "I've just come from Clip 'N' Curl, and they have ruined . . . my . . . hair!"

"Oh, no!" Tracy's hand flew to her mouth. "What did they do?"

"This!" Nora dramatically flung off the pink chiffon scarf, removed her sunglasses, and braced herself for her friends' reactions.

A collective moan went up from Jen and Lucy, and Tracy stared at her in horror. "That bad?" Nora asked grimly.

"It will grow out," Jen said helpfully.

"Or you could buy a wig," Tracy offered.

"Please," Nora said, holding up her hand. "I'll just have to live with it for the next year or so. There's really no other solution, unless I put a bag over my head."

"I saw a movie about that once," Tracy piped up. "It was called *The Man in the Iron Mask*, and this poor man had to wear a big metal thing on his head night and day . . ."

Lucy rolled her eyes in despair. "Tracy, I saw that movie, too. The man in the iron mask had more serious problems than being seen with a bad permanent!"

"Well, there were a lot of similarities," Tracy said defensively.

"Can we please stop talking about hair?" Nora pleaded, just as the pizza arrived. "I want to tell you what happened at Clip 'N' Curl."

"Did you have any luck?" Lucy asked, brightening.

"Yes and no." For the next few minutes, Nora told them about Monsieur André and Mademoiselle Bernice, and the strange phone conversation she had overheard. "So I really don't know if we have enough to go on or not," she finished. "What do you think?"

"I'm not sure," Jen said hesitantly. "Some of the elements are there — the Frenchman, the redhead, the Southern accent. But just a minute," she added, turning to Jen. "I thought the redhead you saw at Temptations was a man."

"I thought it was," Lucy said, shrugging, "but I only saw the top of the person's head. I really can't be sure."

"So it could have been this Bernice woman . . . and that means we're right back where we started," Lucy said, biting into a steaming slice of pizza. "Except in a way, things are even more confusing now. As far as you know, Monsieur André isn't even a Frenchman, right?"

"I'm sure he isn't," Nora agreed. "When he was talking on the phone, he didn't bother with the phony accent. The man's an imposter."

"He certainly is!" Tracy said vigorously. "He's really got a nerve, calling himself a hairdresser." She took another long look at Nora's tangled chestnut mop and made a mental note to never get a permanent.

Jen frowned. "But if he was the man at Temptations that day, why did he bother putting on a French accent? There was no reason to, because as far as he knew, he was among friends. He had no idea anyone was eavesdropping."

"Good point," Lucy said. She fell silent, trying to think through this new bit of information. The case was beginning to look like one of those giant jigsaw puzzles that didn't make sense.

Later, back at Nora's house, Jen sat cross-legged on the bed while Nora made a futile stab at combing out her hair. She had just finished shampooing it and was examining the frizzy mess in the mirror.

"I can't believe it," she moaned. "I've used three conditioners, a finishing rinse, a detangler, and half a can of mousse! It still looks awful — what else can I do?"

"It doesn't look so bad when it's wet," Jen said tactfully. "Why don't you spray it with hot curl lotion, add some styling gel, and then after you set it, you can zap it with spritzer?"

"Good idea," Nora said, plugging in the hot rollers. "I wish I knew if Monsieur André and Mademoiselle Bernice are really involved in the robbery," she went on. "If they're not, then I ruined my hair for nothing. Not to mention the damage to my pocketbook."

"I wondered about that," Jen said sympathetically. "Did they clean you out?"

"I'm afraid so. I'm going to be baby-sitting the Thompson twins for the next ten years to make it up."

They were silent for the next half hour as Nora blow-dried her hair, and then coaxed it onto the hot rollers.

"I wouldn't leave the curlers in too long," Jen cautioned. "Your hair looks like it's a little . . . uh, dry."

"Dry?" Nora snorted. "The Sahara Desert is dry. My hair is . . ." she paused, thinking, "a wasteland!"

She left the curlers in for exactly three minutes, then slowly removed them, watching as her hair reverted to its original frizzy style.

Nora shook her head sadly. "They could use my hair as the basis for a horror movie," she said after a minute.

"Really?" Jen smiled. If Nora was making jokes, things couldn't be that bad.

"I can see it now," Nora said, pointing to the mirror as if she were reading an invisible marquee. *The Permanent That Wouldn't Die.*

Later that night, Steve Crowley called just as Nora was finishing dinner. "Nora, I've been going over some details about the case," he began abruptly, "and I think we're making a big mistake. We're letting our weakest link tackle the toughest assignment."

"Our weakest link?" Nora took a final gulp of milk and stashed the glass in the dishwasher.

"Tracy Douglas," he said flatly. "Now, please don't take this the wrong way, and I wouldn't hurt her feelings for the world."

Nora couldn't help smiling. "I don't think Tracy would appreciate you calling her a weak link," she said slowly, "but I know what you're getting at."

"The bank detail is one of the most important

things we're doing, and I don't know if Tracy can handle it," Steve said.

"Maybe not alone," Nora said thoughtfully.

"What's that?"

"Listen, Steve, I've got a great idea. Why don't you and Tracy scout out the bank together? That way the job will be done right, and Tracy's feelings won't be hurt."

"Sounds good to me," he said with relief in his voice. "Do you want to call her and tell her?"

"Uh. . .why don't you do it?" She didn't want to get into a long conversation with Tracy.

"Okay," he said doubtfully. "Gosh, you don't think she'll get the wrong idea, do you?"

"The wrong idea?"

"That it's like a date, or something."

"Of course not," Nora said firmly. "This isn't a date, this is business. Detective business."

"Oh, and Nora, one more thing."

"Yes?"

"Thanks. You're a genius, you know?"

Nora laughed. "I know."

The phone rang ten minutes later.

"Nora?" Tracy's voice was so high-pitched and excited, she could hardly recognize it. "You're not going to believe what just happened. The most fantastic thing in the whole world, that's what!"

"What happened?" Nora asked.

"Guess who just called and asked me out? Never mind, I'll tell you," Tracy said. "Steve Crowley!"

"Steve Crowley?" Nora asked. Her hand froze as she reached for a spoon. "Tracy, I think you made a mistake. . . ." Didn't she know that Steve only had eyes for Jen?

"No, there's no mistake. It's true," Tracy insisted. "We're going to the bank together on Monday, isn't that super? What do you think I should wear? I can't decide between my new black jumpsuit or my white sweater with the charcoal skirt. And I wondered about my hair — should I wear it pulled back in barrettes, or just set it on hot rollers and let it hang soft and loose? And makeup! I've got that new tawny peach blush but I don't know if it will match my coral lipstick. Gosh," she wailed, "how will I ever get it together by tomorrow? There's so much to think about!"

Nora winced. "Uh, Tracy," she cut in firmly, "before you get too carried away, you and I need to talk."

Chapter 8

"I'm still not sure how we're going to handle this," Jen said nervously to Lucy early the following Monday afternoon. School had let out early for a teachers' meeting. It was one-thirty, and they had returned to Temptations, hoping to get a lead on the identities of the robbers.

"I told you," Lucy replied. "Our best bet is to strike up a conversation with one of the waitresses. That's why I made sure we got the same booth we had the last time." Lucy paused, studying the enormous menu spread out on the table in front of them. "What do you feel like? I'm torn between a 'tropical blitz' and a 'triple zombie.' The blitz has pineapple sauce and mint chocolate chip ice cream, but the zombie has melted marshmallows on top."

Jen hesitated, glancing around the crowded

ice-cream parlor. It was mobbed with kids, and the noise level was as high as the Cedar Groves cafeteria. She thought she caught a glimpse of Jason Anthony's fiery red hair darting among the crowd by the front door, but she couldn't be sure. "Actually, I'm not even hungry," she confessed.

She was feeling queasy, and when she looked at the brightly colored menu, the pictures swam before her eyes. "Maybe I could order something small. . . ." She glanced at her reflection in the gilt-edged mirror hanging on the side wall. She looked ghostly pale, and her eyes were unnaturally bright. Of all the days to be stuck in an ice-cream parlour! Her stomach gave a funny lurch, like she was riding an imaginary elevator that was descending too fast, and she tucked her hands in her lap protectively.

"Something small? You've got to be kidding!" Lucy said, not noticing Jen's discomfort. "I've got news for you. We've got to order something enormous, something that will take a long time to eat. Otherwise how will we have a chance to talk to all the waitresses?" she asked reasonably. She rolled up the sleeves on her tan safari blouse. It was modeled after a bush jacket, with squared-off pockets, wooden buttons, and tabs on the shoulders. Jen knew that it had cost a whole month's allowance, but Lucy looked terrific in it, so she supposed it was worth it.

"It's a shame that there's a new waitress for this section today," Jen said. "What time did you say the regular waitress is coming in?"

"Five o'clock," Lucy said briskly. "So all we have to do is keep eating till then." She scanned the menu thoughtfully, ticking off the items with her long fingernails. "Now let's see, what's the biggest thing we can order. . . . "

Half an hour later, Jen wanted to disappear under the table. She knew that if she had to eat one more mouthful of the gigantic strawberry-banana delight that Lucy had ordered, she would die.

"C'mon, Jen," Lucy urged her. "You're not eating your share." She turned the dish around, so Jen could see the tunnel she had made in her half of the mountainous peaks of ice cream. "Look," she exclaimed, "I'm miles ahead of you."

Jen looked at the sundae and wanted to cry. Lucy was right. She had made hardly a dent in it. "I'm sorry," Jen said. Her voice was almost a groan, but Lucy didn't seem to notice. "What size did you order, anyway?" she complained. "There's no end to this thing." She spooned in another mouthful, trying not to gag as the cloyingly sweet syrup slid down her throat.

"Oh, don't be silly," Lucy said gaily. "I only got the medium-priced one. They call this family-sized."

"Family-sized?" Jen croaked. "*Whose* family — the Marches in *Little Women*?"

"Here's our chance," Lucy said suddenly. "You see that waitress over there? I'm sure she was the one standing at the cashier's station the day we saw the robbers."

"Do you think so?" Jen stared at the blonde woman in the yellow and black aproned uniform. "I'm not sure."

"That's her!" Lucy insisted. "Now the problem is, how can we get her attention?"

"I could pretend to choke and you could do the Heimlich maneuver on me." Actually, Jen felt like she was only seconds away from choking — the strawberry ice cream tasted disgustingly like cough medicine, and she wondered how much more she would be able to take.

"Oh, she's walking away," Lucy said, scrambling out of the booth. "I'd better do something fast."

"What are you — " Jen began, but it was too late. Lucy had already scampered down the aisle and was deep in conversation with the blonde waitress. The waitress looked over at Jen once or twice, and Lucy pointed dramatically to the booth behind them — the one where the robbers had sat. At this point, the waitress shook her head firmly. She obviously didn't remember the robbers or wasn't going to admit to it. Jen plunked her elbows on the table and rested her head in her hands, trying to fight a wave of nausea that swept over her. She didn't want to play detective anymore, she wanted to go home!

A moment later, Lucy swept back into her place. "No luck?" Jen asked. Maybe Lucy would be so discouraged she'd want to leave, she thought hopefully.

"Not yet," Lucy said, "but I'm not giving up without a fight."

"I was afraid of that," Jen moaned softly. "What do we do next?"

Lucy leaned across the table, her brown eyes bright and determined. "We do just what we have been doing . . . we wait!"

"We wait . . . " Jen repeated dully.

"That's right," Lucy said, spooning up another mouthful of strawberry-banana delight. The room was starting to sway a little, and Jen decided she'd better speak up.

"Lucy, I think I'm going to be — "

"Here you go!" a voice interrupted her. It was the blonde waitress, and she slammed another gigantic sundae on the table between them. "One mint avalanche!"

She hurried to another table, leaving Jen temporarily speechless. The enormous dish of green ice cream loomed next to her, so close she could smell a faint herbal odor. Except it didn't smell like mint at all. It reminded her of a pine-scented air freshener that Jeff used in the kitchen sometimes, and she felt her stomach do a gentle somersault. Her hands were clammy and a fine film of perspiration was breaking out on her forehead. Suddenly she didn't care anymore what Lucy thought — she knew there was no way she would be able to eat another bite. "Why in the world did you order another sundae?" she managed to gasp.

"I had to," Lucy said blithely. "It was the only way I could get to talk to the waitress. I told her that we were still hungry, and no one was bothering to take our order — " She stopped as Jen put her napkin to her mouth and dashed down the aisle. "Jen? Are you okay?" she said, puzzled. "Ohmigosh — Jen!"

"I can't believe you fainted at the sight of a sundae," Nora said half an hour later. Jen was stretched out on Nora's bed, and Lucy was sprawled on the battered bean bag chair on the floor.

"I didn't faint, exactly," Jen said weakly.

"You could have fooled me!" Lucy retorted. "When I went in the ladies' room at Temptations you were flat out on the floor with a pile of wet paper towels on your head." She shuddered expressively. "I thought you had been murdered or something!"

"I'm really feeling a lot better," Jen said, struggling to sit up. "And I'm a little embarrassed that I made Lucy bring me over here."

"Don't be silly," Nora insisted. "It would have been crazy to try to make it all the way back to your house." She gently pushed Jen back on the pillow, and tucked the quilt around her. "And don't even think of moving. Just take some more sips of that water, and we'll see how you do."

"Yes, doctor," Jen said, teasing. "I guess I'm your first patient." Everyone knew that Nora's dream was to be a physician and she loved to give medical advice to her friends.

"Just don't sue her for malpractice," Lucy joked. She peered at Jen and nodded, satisfied. "You're looking a lot better now. The color's come back to your cheeks."

"Look, will everybody please stop staring at me?" Jen pleaded. "I'm beginning to feel like a character in a soap opera. Lucy, why don't you tell Nora what you found out at Temptations."

"There's not much to tell," Lucy said ruefully. She stood up and began pacing Nora's room as she talked. As usual, the bedroom was very neat, except for a wild jumble of hair conditioners, sprays, and lotions that cluttered the dresser. Poor Nora, Lucy thought sympathetically. She's still trying to salvage her hair.

"You didn't find a single waitress who remembered the robbers?" Nora asked in a discouraged tone. "I guess it was a long shot, anyway."

"They either have rotten memories, or they're covering for someone," Lucy said. "I suppose I could make another trip back there," she said doubtfully. "Jen got sick before I got a chance to talk to the waitress who was due in at five."

"I don't know if it's worth it," Nora said.

"Why don't you wait and see how the other leads work out?"

"What other leads?" Lucy made a face. "We've come up with zilch today!"

"You're not the only investigators in the field, you know," Nora joked. "We have two detectives at work right now."

"We do?"

Nora nodded and explained about Steve Crowley joining Tracy Douglas for the "bank detail." "I just hope she can keep her mind on her work," she muttered.

At that moment, Tracy was hurrying along, ducking her head against the light breeze that was ruffling her hair. She was half an hour late for her appointment to meet Steve, and she could only hope that he wouldn't be too angry.

The afternoon was going to be perfect — she just knew it! She smiled, remembering Nora cautioning her not to think of her assignment with Steve as a date. Nora was sweet, but she was very naive about boys, Tracy thought smugly. Just because he was dating Jen didn't mean he was *immune* to other girls, she thought. She would never do anything to hurt Jen, but Steve wouldn't have suggested that they go to the bank together if he wasn't interested in her.

She glanced down at her new apricot sweater and black wool skirt. Thank goodness she had decided to dash home after school and change, she thought. Today everything had to be perfect. What was that saying they always put on posters and bumper stickers — TODAY IS THE FIRST DAY OF THE REST OF YOUR LIFE. It's true, she thought, giggling with pleasure. She felt like her whole life would start the moment she met Steve in front of the bank.

Five minutes later, she wasn't so sure. Steve was pacing angrily back and forth on the sidewalk, and he greeted Tracy's bubbly hello with a curt nod. Tracy was puzzled — if she didn't know better, she would think he was *annoyed*!

"You're late," he said brusquely. He glanced at his watch. "At least half an hour."

"Well, I had a lot to do," Tracy answered. She moved away from the bank awning, so the bright sun would pick up the highlights in her flaxen hair. "It's not every day I get to — "

"Never mind," Steve interrupted her. "Let's just get this over with."

Get this over with? Tracy's forehead puckered in a frown. Steve hadn't said a word about her terrific sweater and skirt or the way her hair looked. She had experimented with a new style, sweeping her hair back into a sleek French braid, with soft fluffy bangs, and she had added a tiny velvet bow. And the makeup! She had spent forty-five minutes in front of the mirror the night before, testing four shades of smoky blue eyeshadow before she was satisfied. Why didn't he say anything? Didn't he notice?

"There are a couple of ways we can approach this," he was saying in his husky voice. "We can separate once we get in the lobby, and one of us can talk to the teller while the other one. . . ." Tracy tuned out the rest of what he was saying, because she was too busy looking at his broad shoulders. He looked like the ideal American boy, she thought, with his clear blue eyes, and that cute spike of dark brown hair that kept falling over one eye. She couldn't help staring at him — no wonder Jen was crazy about him! They were standing so close she could see a sprinkling of freckles on Steve's nose, and she noticed that his teeth were white and even, like someone in a toothpaste commercial. But of course there was Jen . . . who was her friend. What a problem!

She wondered if he was a good dancer, and

decided that he probably was. If he ever really asked her out, what would she wear?

"What do you think of the plan so far?" Steve asked, suddenly jolting her back to reality.

"The plan?" Tracy wondered how long she had been tuned out.

"To get information out of the tellers," he said impatiently.

"I think it sounds wonderful," she said. She'd heard that boys loved it when you agreed with them, so she fixed him with her big blue eyes, and tried to look impressed. "You're a genius, Steve." She waited patiently for him to say something nice about her, but he just stared absently at the traffic whizzing by, apparently lost in thought.

"I just hope we don't mess this up," he said after a moment. "I guess what worries me is that we'll only get one shot at checking out the bank. If we come back a second time, it will really look suspicious."

"Of course we're not going to mess it up," Tracy said, tapping him playfully on the arm. She laughed softly, but she might have been talking to a statue. He actually seemed *serious* about all this, she thought incredulously. Could it be that he really believed Nora's crazy story about overhearing the details of a bank heist?

As far as she was concerned, Nora, Jen, and Lucy could have dreamed the whole thing up as a giant joke; and even if it was true, why should they get involved? Let the police handle it, that was their job — to protect the people. . . .

"If I were a bank robber, I'd never pick this place to rob," Steve said suddenly. "You'd be stuck once you got outside — you'd have to escape on foot."

"Why?" Tracy looked up and down the street. "There's plenty of room to park a car out front. Maybe even two cars."

"But this is a towaway zone," Steve pointed out. "See that painted yellow line? Anyway, the getaway car is supposed to be parked in front of Clip 'N' Curl."

"But that's miles away and it's in the mall."

"I know." He frowned, scratching his chin. "This case is getting crazier by the minute. They must be going to use two getaway cars. It's the only thing that makes sense."

"Why would they do that?"

"To throw the police off the trail," he said. "They did that on *Magnum P. I.* once." He paused, studying the yellow line again. "They're still taking a big chance, though. Why would a bank robber want to park his getaway car in a towaway zone? Think of all the attention it would attract — plus it might even get towed away!"

"Mmm, that never occurred to me," Tracy said, sounding thoughtful. If she had to listen to one more word about this stupid bank robbery, she was going to scream! Why were they still standing out in the middle of the sidewalk, anyway? she wondered. She was dying to get inside. Her feet were killing her — she had worn her new black pumps to go with the skirt — and worse, the wind was ruining her bangs. "Uh, Steve," she said cautiously, "do you think we should go inside now?"

"Sure," he agreed. "We've scouted out the street as much as we can." He turned toward the double glass doors that led to the bank lobby and stopped. "Any questions?"

"Well, just a little one," she said in her whispery voice.

"What's that?"

"What am I supposed to do once we get inside?"

Chapter 9

"What makes Jen think this could be an inside job?" Steve whispered a couple of minutes later. They were standing in the lobby of the Cedar Groves Savings and Trust, trying to look inconspicuous.

"Oh, I don't know," Tracy said sullenly. Jen, Jen — she was tired of hearing about Jen! "Maybe she overheard something that day at Temptations, or maybe she's just guessing." Who cares? she added silently. She was already sick of the entire project, and Steve had turned out to be a major disappointment. If he had any interest in her as a girlfriend, he was doing a terrific job of hiding it, she thought disgustedly. She glanced around the bank and wondered if there was a ladies' room where she could touch up her hair.

"Okay, now do you know what to do?" Steve interrupted her thoughts.

"I'm supposed to check out the number of security guards and the location of the vault," she said in a bored voice.

"Right," Steve said approvingly. "And then if you have any time left over, try to strike up a conversation with one of the tellers. And do you remember the three things you're supposed to look for?"

"Gosh, what is this — a pop quiz?" Tracy shifted uncomfortably on her high heels, while she wracked her brain trying to think of what Steve wanted her to say. Finally she remembered. "I should watch out for a Southern accent, a French accent, and someone with red hair."

"Good girl." Steve gave her a dazzling smile, and just for a second, Tracy forgot she was supposed to be mad at him. How could anyone who looked so great be such a total loss as a boyfriend? It was obvious he had no romantic interest in her. Good girl! she thought grimly. That's probably the same thing he says to his cocker spaniel!

"You're sure you'll be okay?"

"I'm positive," Tracy snapped. "Let's get going."

"Good idea. We're attracting too much attention just by standing here. When you're done, meet me at Temptations."

Tracy brightened. "You want to go to Temptations?" she said delightedly. She smiled up at him, her blue eyes glowing. Surely he didn't consider Temptations part of the assignment. Maybe there was hope after all!

"To compare notes," he said briefly. "That way we can summarize everything before we have to give a report to Nora."

"Oh." So much for *that* fantasy! Tracy thought. A moment later, he nodded and moved off toward the row of glass-walled offices in the back of the bank. Tracy knew he had some vague plan of talking with one of the bank executives. She had no idea how he was going to manage that, but he seemed so annoyingly confident that she didn't doubt him for a minute. Anyway, she had her own problems to worry about.

She glanced around the lobby, considering her next move. The bank was one of Cedar Groves's oldest buildings, and the executives had decided to keep the same old-fashioned decor it had back in 1900. As far as Tracy was concerned, it was a crazy idea, but a lot of people seemed to like the dark mahogany furniture, potted palms, and wrought-iron teller's cages. They even had kept the original gaslight fixtures mounted on the wall, except now they were fitted with light bulbs. Tracy was staring at a display case filled with memorabilia — dusty old account books and faded yellow ledgers — when a voice behind her made her jump.

"They really knew how to write in those days, didn't they?"

She turned to see a middle-aged security guard standing next to her. He was staring fondly at the collection in the glass case, his ruddy face creased in a broad smile. "Penmanship, that was the thing," he went on. "Look at those letters, you can tell they were done with a quill pen."

Tracy peered obediently down at one of the ledger books, wondering what the big deal was about. So they wrote neatly back in 1900 — so what? What else did they have to do? Television hadn't even been invented! "It's very nice," she said politely.

"Nice? It's a work of art. Yessir, a work of art." He was obviously waiting for Tracy to agree with him, so she nodded her head with as much enthusiasm as she could muster. "They used the Palmer Method — I don't suppose you study that in school anymore."

"Uh, no, we don't," Tracy said. She was about to move away from the display case and the talkative man when suddenly she realized she had stumbled on a potential gold mine. The man was a security guard! What incredible luck! She could pump him for tons of information about the bank, certainly enough to impress Steve.

"Have you been working as a security guard for a long time?" Tracy asked, putting on her brightest voice. It was important to strike up a good rapport with him, and she flashed her most dazzling smile.

"Well, let me see." The old man stared thoughtfully at the ceiling as if the answer would magically appear in the creamy white plaster. "I started as a guard in the summer of '62. . . ."

Sixty-two! Tracy thought, I wasn't even born yet. "You must really like your job," she gushed. "Even though I'm sure it must be very demanding." She knew exactly how she would play this. She would gain his confidence, and then find out all about the bank security system. She could just picture herself giving a full report to Steve. He would be amazed that she had accomplished so much, but she would just smile modestly and tell him it was nothing.

"Well, it has its moments," he said thoughtfully. "But you have to take the bad with the good, you know."

"Oh, absolutely." Tracy nodded seriously as though he had just said something very profound. "But it must be really demanding," she repeated, wishing he would get the hint. "It must take a lot of your energy and time."

"It's the kind of job that keeps you on your toes," he said, flattered. "You can't goof off, if you're a security guard, you know. Things can happen just like that." He snapped his fingers, his expression solemn. "One minute everything's quiet, and the next, it's a madhouse."

"Oh, I can imagine." Tracy glanced around, looking for Steve. He was nowhere in sight, so she supposed he had managed to talk to one of the bank officers. She wondered what tack to try next. The security guard was going to need a lot of encouragement — he had an amazing ability to talk a lot and say absolutely nothing.

He started another monologue about the items in the display case, and Tracy listened absently, hoping she didn't look as bored as she felt. She tried to think of the most important points she should ask about. Steve wanted to know as much as he could about bank security, so she supposed she should find out how the bank was guarded at night. Was there an alarm system, or maybe an electric eye? Were the guards on duty all night, or did police patrol the building? She wondered if the police had assigned extra officers to the bank after Nora's trip to the station house, but she doubted it. From what Nora had said, no one had taken her very seriously.

After ten minutes had passed, Tracy finally got the nerve to break into his rambling conversation. "I've always been interested in electronics," she said enthusiastically. "And I was wondering," she hesitated, choosing her words carefully, "what exactly would happen if someone broke in here at night? Would a buzzer go off at the police station? Or would the bank vault automatically close and seal the robbers inside?"

He peered at her suspiciously. "Well now, that seems a funny thing to be asking about."

Tracy thought fast. "Yes, I suppose it does. But I'm writing a short story for English class," she said, "and the main character is a bank robber. It's a thriller," she added proudly.

"Hmm, that's different," he admitted. "Well, I certainly wish I could help you, but I don't know a thing about the security system here."

"You don't?" Tracy wailed. Her fantasy

scene at Temptations — the one where Steve was so impressed by her — shattered into a million pieces. "But you said you've been here for years. Since 1962."

"No, I said I've been a security guard for years," he corrected her. "I used to work at the Capwell Factory out on Route One — the place they make chicken nuggets." He paused as a voice crackled over his walkie-talkie. "Have to go," he said, lifting the device to his ear. "I don't want to make a bad impression my first day on the job."

"Your first day on the job?" Tracy said in disbelief. He turned and ambled across the lobby then, and she felt like sitting on the cold marble floor and crying. She had failed at her assignment, and Steve would never understand!

"I don't understand," Steve said irritably half an hour later. They were sitting at Temptations, sipping chocolate sodas. "Why were you talking to someone who guards chicken nuggets? You were supposed to be investigating the security system at the bank."

"Well, I was," Tracy protested. "At least I thought I was," she amended. She glanced at herself in the mirror — her face was flushed and her once-sleek French braid was trailing sadly down her back. My hair looks as limp as I feel, she said silently. Plus she had developed two enormous blisters on her heels from her new black pumps, and she had snagged her designer hose. She sighed unhappily and leaned back in the booth. Whoever would have thought that detective work could take so much out of you?

"Run that by me again," Steve ordered. "You thought he worked for the bank, but he didn't?"

"He did work for the bank," Tracy began. "He was wearing a security guard uniform and I was really excited when he struck up a conversation with me. I figured he was the lead we were looking for."

"But?"

Tracy shrugged. "But it was his first day at work, so naturally, he didn't have any information for me."

"Why didn't you dump him and move on to someone else?" Steve had finished his soda and was looking enviously at hers.

"I couldn't. I spent so long buttering him up. . ." Tracy paused, wondering if she had said too much, "that I just ran out of time."

Steve exhaled slowly. "Well," he said finally,

"I'm not sure I did any better than you did, to be honest."

"Really?" Tracy felt like breaking out into a grin. Steve couldn't possibly be angry with her, if he failed, too. They were both in the same boat! "I thought I saw you disappear into one of the offices at the back."

"I made an appointment to see the loan officer," Steve told her. "I told him I wanted to take out a loan to buy a car, and asked him what my chances were."

"Wow," Tracy said, clearly impressed. "What did he say?"

Steve laughed, and signaled the waitress for another soda. "Well, first he asked me if I could drive. And then when he found out how old I was, he suggested that I join the Christmas Club," he said ruefully.

"Oh, no," Tracy giggled. She looked up at the clock on the wall and gasped. It was getting late, and unless she did something fast, they would soon be separating, heading home to dinner. She wouldn't get to see him again until the next meeting at Nora's and that wasn't scheduled for a whole week!

"Penny for your thoughts," Steve said suddenly. "You look like you're a million miles away."

Tracy was stunned. It was the first thing Steve had said to her that wasn't directly related to the investigation. She struggled to make the most of it. "I was just thinking of the case," she said, hoping she sounded convincing. "Do you think we should try to make another trip to the bank tomorrow?" she asked hopefully. "Maybe I could do better the second time around."

"No, I think we've gotten as much information as we can. I forgot to tell you. I did hear one Southern accent, and I saw one man with red hair . . . plus I got a pretty good look at the door that leads to the vault and the safe deposit boxes." He paused as the waitress put another soda down in front of him. "What's Nora going to do with all this information anyway?"

"I don't know," Tracy said honestly. "I guess she figures that once she gets all the reports in, she'll have enough to go back to Captain Simpson."

Steve sipped his soda thoughtfully. "I hope the other teams have done better than we have," he said wryly. "We're sure not giving her much to go on."

"I think she'll understand we did the best we could," Tracy replied, looking properly serious.

She had certainly done the best she could, she thought ironically. She had done everything in the world to make Steve notice her, and had failed miserably. She guessed he really *was* madly in love with Jen!

Chapter 10

"I don't understand," Susan Hillard said nastily. It was the following Friday night and Nora had called a general meeting in her basement. "You spent twenty minutes in the Cedar Groves Savings and Trust, and you didn't come up with *anything*?" The whole group was gathered in Nora's basement watching as Susan and Tracy battled it out.

"I didn't say that," Tracy retaliated. "You're putting words in my mouth."

"I wish I could put brains in your head," Susan said, getting a laugh from Tommy Ryder.

Lucy, who had taken up a position by the Ping-Pong table, raised her hands for silence. She looked calm and in control, but inwardly, she was seething! The whole meeting was getting out of hand, she thought. Everyone was talking at once — and criticizing each other's efforts — and nothing was getting accomplished.

"Look," she said, raising her voice enough to cut through the laughter, "Tracy's not on trial here. I'm sure she did the best she could at the bank."

"Yeah," Susan chortled. "If we ever hear about any chicken nuggets escaping, we'll know who to contact."

"I told you," Tracy said, her blue eyes filling with tears, "I didn't know that he spent his whole life at a nugget factory. I thought he had always been a bank guard."

"Look, Susan," Steve called out from the back of the room, "let's not waste time dumping on Tracy. The main thing is that we all pull together and try to find a link in these progress reports."

Tracy flashed a grateful smile, but Susan said rudely, "I knew he'd take Tracy's side. He's a sucker for blonde hair and blue eyes," she said to Jennifer, who was sitting next to her. Jen looked stricken. What was Susan talking about?

"A link? He's looking for a link?" Tommy Ryder hooted. "Hey, what about Andy Warwick? He's a *missing* link!"

"You're just lucky he's not here tonight, you little creep," Mia Stevens yelled. "You'd be dead meat!" Mia was sprawled on a pile of cushions, her long legs stretched out in front of her. She was wearing black textured hose, and Jen couldn't help staring at the strange design running up and down her legs. Jen knew it was supposed to be the *fleur-de-lis* pattern, because she had been with Mia when she bought them, but in the dim light of the basement, Mia looked like she was covered with hundreds of little black ants!

"Yeah, I'm really scared," Tommy said, grinning. He staggered backward in mock horror, stumbling into his friend Mitch Pauley, who grunted and gave him a good-natured shove.

Lucy checked her notes and sighed, wondering how she could inject a little order into the meeting. So far, every lead had turned out to be a dead end, and the group was getting restless. If she wasn't careful, it was going to end up as a free-for-all. She glanced toward the food table — at least the pizza bites were holding out, she thought. Probably because Jason Anthony had missed the meeting. She glanced over the audience, and decided to call on Steve Crowley next. He was bound to have something encouraging to report.

"I'm afraid I don't have much that's encouraging," he said a moment later, eliciting a loud groan from the group. He had walked to the front of the room, and seemed completely at ease, his hands thrust deep into the pockets of his khaki pants.

"Don't tell me you got sidetracked by the nugget king, too," Susan Hillard blurted out. "I thought only Tracy was that gullible."

"No, I didn't get sidetracked," he replied, ignoring her insults. He turned to Lucy. "I did the assignment, but I didn't get any terrific leads. Sorry about that."

"That's okay," Lucy said, trying not to look as discouraged as she felt. "Did you get a chance to talk to the bank employees?"

"A few, but none of them looked suspicious. I did hear a Southern accent, and I spotted one man with red hair, but apart from that. . . ." He shrugged and raised his hands in a hopeless gesture. "Oh, and I got a look at the bank vault, and the safe deposit boxes. I can't imagine how anyone's going to get in there. The door looks like it's about three feet thick."

"Wow," Nora said softly, "we really are back

to square one." She was busily refilling paper cups with cola and stopped to glance at Steve. "Are you saving the good news for last, by any chance? You took the drinking glass over to the lab, didn't you?"

"I sure did, but there's no good news there, either," Steve said slowly. "They couldn't lift any prints off it."

"Oh, no," Jen piped up. She scrambled to her feet and joined Lucy in the front of the room. She was determined to find something optimistic to say. "Look," she began, "does anybody have anything else to report? Anything at all," she added, looking at her friends.

Lucy bit her lip. "Well, I wasn't going to say anything, but I had some evidence analyzed without telling anybody."

"You did?" Jen asked, her eyes wide with surprise. "What evidence?"

"The chocolate chip cookie," she said a little sheepishly. "I took it to my sister's orthodontist, and he said he'd try to analyze it for free. You know, for bite marks."

"Really?" Jen was impressed. "What did he say?"

"He said that whoever ate that chocolate chip cookie has a Class Four overbite."

"But what does that *mean*?" Jen asked excitedly.

"It means he — or she — can eat a sandwich through a Venetian blind," Tommy Ryder chortled. "See, like this!" He sucked in his cheeks and drew his lips over his teeth to imitate someone with an overbite.

"He's right," Lucy said reluctantly. "All it tells us is that the person had an overbite, and it's a pretty common type. It probably wouldn't help make a positive identification, or anything like that." She paused. "I'm afraid that about does it for the reports," she said, scanning her sheet. "We've already heard from Nora. . . ."

"Yeah, I meant to tell you, Nora — nice hair!" Susan Hillard chuckled. "I hope you don't touch any more live wires."

Nora flushed angrily and self-consciously touched her tight chestnut curls. She had worked on her hair for a whole hour before the meeting, and she was darned if she was going to put up with any nasty remarks from Susan! "Look , you little — "

"Let's not get carried away," Lucy said hastily. She glared at Susan and waited until the room was quiet once more. "We've brought you up-to-date on everything we've done so far.

Now, does anybody have any new ideas? We're open to suggestions."

"Yeah," Mitch Pauley said, shuffling to his feet. "Can we rent a video? They have *Police Academy III* down at Video Biz. . . ."

"I meant, suggestions about the crime," Lucy said curtly.

"Who wants to rent a video? Let's take a vote," Tommy Ryder suggested. He jumped up on the seat of his chair, waving his arms enthusiastically. "C'mon, let's see a show of hands!"

Lucy looked on helplessly as a chorus of applause went up. The meeting was disintegrating, right before her very eyes, and unless a miracle occurred. . . .

"Relax everybody, I'm here!"

Every head turned to see Jason Anthony careening down the basement steps. He was dressed in jeans and an army green camouflage T-shirt, his red hair disheveled. He paused dramatically on the stairs, smiling and waving like a celebrity greeting his fans.

"Please, no autographs tonight. I'm exhausted," he said, lifting his hand weakly to his forehead. "Perhaps if one of you will be kind enough to get me something cold to drink . . . "

"You're late, Jason," Lucy said crisply.

"We've already gone through everyone's statements."

"Yeah, and you didn't miss a thing," Mitch Pauley assured him. "It's been zilch, zip, and zero. Nobody had anything to report, and we're just about to rent a video. How does *Police Academy III* sound to you?"

Jason swung himself athletically over the banister and landed close to Susan Hillard, who shuddered and tried to move away. "Did you miss me? I got here as quickly as I could," he said, leering into her face.

"Get away from me," she said, jumping to her feet. She grabbed her pocketbook and headed for the stairs. "Thanks for another pointless evening," she hurled over her shoulder to Lucy. "As usual, nothing was accomplished. Talk about a total waste of time," she muttered, hurrying up the stairs.

Jason waited until he heard the sound of the front door slamming, and then grinned from ear to ear. "What a shame," he said, piling up a handful of pizza bites on a paper plate. "Now she'll never know that I've solved the crime."

For a moment, there was dead silence, and then Nora sprang to life. "You what? You solved the crime?" she gasped. "What happened? What did you find out?"

"Oh, this and that," Jason said, collapsing into a recliner. "Now, if someone would just get me a cold drink. . . ."

"Forget about a drink," Lucy said, moving toward him. "What do you know, Jason?"

"Ah, he doesn't know anything," Tommy Ryder sneered. "It's just his way of getting attention."

"Geniuses are always misunderstood," Jason murmured. He picked up the remote control and flicked on the television. "Ah, *Dallas*," he said. "Does someone want to fill me in on the plot? What does J. R. *really* want?"

"Jason," Nora said threateningly. "If you know something, you've got to tell us now. There isn't a moment to lose."

"No?" he asked, his mouth full of pizza. "What's the rush?"

"The rush is that you only have three minutes to live," Lucy said, standing over him. She gave him her sweetest smile. She yanked the remote away from him, and grabbed him by the shirt front. "Let's try a little experiment. Let's see how long you can live without air."

"Hey," Jason said, pushing her away. "Is this any way to treat your top detective?"

"Top detective!" Mitch Pauley snorted. "You

couldn't find a criminal if you. . . ." He paused, thinking.

"If you tripped over one!" Tommy Ryder finished for him.

"That's great," Jason said approvingly. "Two bodies and one brain." He turned to Nora. "I can't talk when my mouth is dry. I'm so parched, I can just feel the words wilting away." He smiled winningly as Nora glowered and handed him a cola. "Ah," he said, drinking noisily. "Now I can give my report.'"

"Give it," Lucy snapped. "What exactly do you know, Jason? And no tricks. I want the truth." She glared at him, wondering if he really had come up with something valuable. It seemed incredible that Jason could stumble across the identity of the robbers, but anything was possible.

"I was at the mall," he began. He looked around the room, waiting for someone to interrupt him, but they sensed something important was about to happen, and no one spoke.

"You were at the mall," Nora said, urging him on. "And what?"

"Well, I was strolling by Guido's, you know, that store that has the expensive exercise clothes?"

"Oh, I love that store," Tracy said. "They have the cutest running suit you ever saw. It's bright peach, and it has a gray suede collar with little pearl buttons on the cuffs — " She stopped suddenly as Lucy crept up behind her and placed her hand over Tracy's mouth.

"Please continue, Jason," Lucy said firmly.

"And I was killing time waiting for my mother, so I decided to check out the running shoes in the window." He paused like an actor. "And that's when I saw them."

"That's when you saw what?" Nora asked.

"A pair of Riveaus," he said calmly, "Gray and black, just like Jen described."

"Ohmigosh!" Tracy yelped, pulling Lucy's hand away from her mouth. "Who was wearing them?"

"No one was wearing them," Lucy said wearily. "He saw them in the window. On display, right?"

"Right." Jason paused to refill his cola, while everyone stared at him. "I walked inside," he went on, "and talked to the salesman. I pretended to be interested in the Riveaus, and he told me they only had one pair in stock. The pair in the window."

"Were they your size?" Tracy asked, interested.

"*Tracy*, he wasn't going to buy them, he was just trying to find out information about them!" Nora thundered.

"You don't have to be so touchy," Tracy complained.

"Luckily they weren't my size," Jason told her. "But I found out something really interesting. The gray and black ones are really unusual, and Guido's is the only store that carries them." He paused to let this sink in. "And here's the good part. The salesman remembered he had one other pair in stock, but someone sold them last month."

"Wow," Lucy said. "Who bought them?"

Jason shook his head. "He doesn't know. Apparently, a part-time clerk sold them."

"But he sold them to a man, right?" Nora asked.

"Not necessarily. They have the same style and color for women, you know."

"Jen," Nora said hurriedly, "we never even thought of that. Could a woman have been wearing those Riveaus you saw in the aisle at Temptations?"

Jen nodded slowly. "Definitely. I don't know why we didn't think of it before."

"Wait, there's more," Jason said, drawing the conversation back to himself. "The salesman gave me another tip. He said most of his customers who wear Riveaus are exercise nuts — they spend all their time at Great Bodies."

"The health spa on Baker Street," Lucy offered. "Fantastic!" she said, snapping her fingers. "Jason, I hate to say it, but I think you're on to something. Maybe you really are a genius!"

Jason stood up, grinning, and gave a theatrical bow. "If that's a compliment," he said grandly, "I accept."

"Now," Lucy said briskly, "who wants to check out Great Bodies?"

Chapter 11

"I still think there's too many of us," Lucy grumbled the next day. It was a bright, clear Saturday morning, and she and Tracy were at the Twin Rivers Mall, waiting for Jen and Steve to meet them at Great Bodies.

"But you said you could get us in for free on a guest pass," Tracy pointed out. "And besides, we're going to need all the help we can get. We'll need Steve to cover the men's half of the gym and — "

"Tracy," Lucy said patiently, "I hate to disillusion you, but there isn't any 'men's' half of the gym. This is a unisex spa. That's why my parents joined — they wanted to be able to spend some time together while they exercised."

"A unisex spa?" Tracy wrinkled her nose and

carefully inspected her fingernails. She had tried a new shade of polish to match her bright plum running suit, and she still felt a little uncertain about the color. "What does that mean exactly?" Her little-girl voice was suspicious.

"That means that all the classes are coed. The aerobics, the Nautilus equipment, the running track. . .everything is used by men and women together."

Tracy stared at her in horror. "You mean there's going to be boys there, watching us . . . as we sweat? How utterly gross! Why didn't someone tell me?" she said plaintively.

"What difference does it make?" Lucy asked. "You're not here to meet boys," she added sternly. "You're here to do detective work, re-. member?" She stared at Tracy in her designer running suit and carefully styled hair. It was obvious that she never should have been assigned to the project, Lucy thought.

"Well, honestly, Lucy, you don't have to snap at me," Tracy objected. "I know the reason I'm here."

Tracy saw Steve and immediately started waving her arms. "Hey, we're over here!" she shouted.

Lucy grabbed her arm. "Quiet!" she ordered. "We need to keep a low profile, not alert half the mall that we're here." Lucy checked her watch as Jen and Steve approached. Nine-forty-five. Perfect timing, she thought. Her mother said that Saturday morning was the busiest time at the spa, and that the ten o'clock aerobics class was the most popular.

Lucy's eyes skimmed over Steve's and Jen's outfits. They were wearing almost identical navy blue running suits with blue and white running shoes. Their exercise clothes were practical, rather than eye-catching like Tracy's — and she was glad to see that both of them had remembered to bring gym bags. When they planned the day's strategy at Nora's kitchen table, she had warned them to be prepared for everything from weight-lifting to Jacuzzis. It was nice to know they had taken her seriously.

"Are we late?" Steve said a moment later. "We stopped to get muffins and orange juice on the way over here."

"You're fine," Lucy assured him. She pushed open the glass doors to Great Bodies and ushered them inside. "I'm not sure that the muffin was a good idea, though." Loud rock music pulsed through the lobby, and she had to raise her voice to be heard. "I always come here on an empty stomach."

"Really? Why?"

Lucy smiled mysteriously as they approached the reception desk. "This is the toughest spa in town," she said. "It's a real no-nonsense place. High-energy aerobics, and what they call state-of-the-art weight-lifting equipment. The people here really take their exercise seriously."

"I can see that," Tracy said, peering in at a glass-walled room filled with shiny steel equipment. She saw dozens of sweating bodies strapped to machines, struggling to lift heavy weights, and she backed a little closer to Lucy. "They look like they're in pain!" she whispered.

"You know what they say — no pain, no gain!" Steve teased. "Don't worry, Tracy," he said, punching her lightly on the arm, "I'll check out the weight-lifting room if you want. I've used Nautilus equipment before, so I won't look out of place."

"Just don't get hurt," Tracy said nervously. She took another look, just in time to see a skinny blonde girl lift a barbell that looked heavier than she was. The girl braced her feet wide apart, and suddenly lifted the barbell chest high, every muscle in her neck bulging. "How yucky," Tracy said. "It's a torture chamber in there."

"C'mon, Tracy, pull yourself together," Lucy said. "The quicker we get registered, the quicker we can start looking for that pair of Riveaus."

"And the quicker we can get out of here!" Tracy murmured feelingly.

Moments later, Tracy, Lucy, and Jen found themselves walking down a long hallway, following the sounds of the pulsating rock music. "I thought we'd scout out some of the aerobics classes," Lucy suggested, "and then we can take a look at the steam room and the sauna."

"What about Steve?" Tracy said worriedly. "Do you think he'll be okay back there?" They had left him in the Nautilus room, and he was being coached by a burly instructor who looked like he had just escaped from an Arnold Schwarzenegger movie.

"He'll be fine," Jen said crisply. Tracy was acting far too interested in Steve's welfare! "We'll see him back in the lobby when this is all over."

"If we ever get out of here alive," Tracy muttered, peering into one of the rooms. "These people must want to kill themselves . . . ohmigosh!" She stopped so suddenly that Nora and Lucy nearly tripped over her. "That's it. I mean that's them!"

"What?" Jen asked, peering over her shoulder. She stared at a sea of whirling bodies in bright leotards and leg warmers. Since it was a coed class, there was also a sprinkling of navy blue gym shorts and white T-shirts, an outfit popular with the men.

"The shoes — the Riveaus!" Tracy gasped. "Look — they're right over . . . oh, no! They've gone." She took a step inside the room, trying to shade her eyes against the dizzying, colored strobe lights that played across the floor. The music suddenly picked up in tempo, and to her horror, it seemed like the whole class was advancing toward her in a wave of Spandex!

"Tracy, watch out!" Jen pulled her back into the hall. "Did you really see them? They're probably lots of Riveaus, but the ones we're looking for are black and gray with suede trim."

"I saw them, I'm sure of it," Tracy said, leaning weakly against the wall. Her face was a sickly white color, and her hands were trembling. "It seems scary to think that we've finally come face-to-face with one of the robbers."

"Well, we're not face-to-face with him yet," Lucy said dubiously. She hated to sound so suspicious, but she knew that Tracy had a vivid imagination. And it seemed pretty darn unlikely that they'd walk into Great Bodies and find the Riveaus in the first five minutes! "Tracy," she began, "are you absolutely sure of what you saw? You know sometimes when you *want* to see something, your mind plays tricks on you, and you *imagine* you see it."

"I'm telling you, I saw them!" Tracy said stubbornly. "You believe me, don't you, Jen?"

"Of course I do," Jen said, after hesitating for a moment. "There's just one thing that puzzles me. Lucy," she said thoughtfully, "you said we're not face-to-face with *him* yet. Are we still assuming that it's a man wearing those Riveaus?"

Lucy stared at her in surprise. "Gosh, I didn't even think to ask. Tracy, how about it? Who was wearing them — a man or a woman?"

"I . . . I don't know," the blonde girl said helplessly.

Lucy raised her eyebrows. "You don't *know?*"

"I can't be *sure* if it was a man or a woman." Tracy tilted her chin defiantly. "All I know is that someone in that aerobics class is wearing the shoes we're looking for." She glanced nervously into the room. The group had advanced toward the mirror and was doing some sort of complicated dance step to a Mick Jagger song.

Their feet were moving so quickly it was impossible to get a good look at their footwear, and Tracy shook her head in despair. It was maddening to come so close, and then have this happen! She knew from the skeptical expression on Lucy's face that she thought she had invented the whole thing. "It's no use, I can't spot them anymore. The colored lights, the strobes — everything is just a blur in there," she said apologetically.

"Tracy, try to think!" Lucy hissed. "What did you see above the shoes?"

"Um, socks, I guess. Yeah, light gray ones," she said brightening.

"I mean *above* the socks," Lucy insisted. "Did you see tights, or bare legs or — "

"I told you I can't remember," Tracy snapped. "I only saw them for a split second and — oh, no! There they are!" She pointed toward a cluster of gyrating bodies that were moving in rhythm to Michael Jackson's new hit.

"Where?" Jen asked excitedly.

"They've disappeared!" Tracy wailed.

"Here we go again!" Lucy said, rolling her eyes.

"C'mon," Tracy said, a determined look on her delicate face. She linked arms with Jen and Lucy, her blue eyes glinting. "Enough is enough! I'm not letting those Riveaus get away from me again!" Before they could object, she pulled the girls into the dimly lit room and they were immediately enveloped by a tide of swaying bodies.

It was like swimming upstream against a school of salmon, Jen thought. The mirrored room was more than crowded, it was packed with bodies, and she struggled to stake out a spot for herself near her friends. She yelped in pain as a stray elbow jabbed her in the ribs, and inched a little closer to Lucy, who was doing her best to follow the complicated routine the group was doing.

"Hey, get with it, you guys!" The instructor was screaming over the heavy drumbeat. "Heel, toe, heel, turn and clap. You can do it!"

"Easy for her to say," Jen muttered. Arms flailing, she tried desperately to match her arm and leg movements to the instructor, who was dancing vigorously on a small platform at the front of the room. She was a woman in her early twenties, wearing a bright yellow leotard that looked like it had been painted on her slim body. She must be in terrific condition, Jen thought enviously, because she wasn't even sweating like the rest of the class!

"Hmm . . ." Lucy muttered. "I have an idea."

"What is it?" Jen said, moving closer to her friend. She wondered why Lucy's voice sounded so funny — as if an elephant was sitting on her chest — and then she realized that she sounded the same way.

"I think . . . I think," Lucy paused, gulping in air as they began a series of jumping jacks.

"Yes? You think what?" Jen croaked. They'd only been in class a few minutes but her pulse was racing and her lungs felt ready to explode. If Lucy didn't hurry up, she wouldn't live long enough to hear what she had to say!

"I think . . . we . . . should . . . divide up the room." She took another long breath before throwing herself from left to right in a series of lunges.

Divide up the room? Divide up the room? Jen had no idea what she was talking about, but from the look on Lucy's face, she was in no shape to explain. Jen sighed and started the leg lunges, her thighs rebelling every inch of the way. "Oh, I get it!" she said suddenly. She smiled, and flashed Lucy an okay sign with thumb and forefinger touching.

Of course! They could divide up the room in thirds, that way they would make sure they didn't miss the Riveaus. "I'll take the right . . ."

Jen gasped to Lucy . . . "and you stay where you are in the middle." After what seemed like an eternity, she gathered enough breath to say, "Tell Tracy to take the left."

Lucy nodded, apparently not trusting herself to speak, and Jen moved off to the right wall, which was mirrored from top to bottom. She glanced at her reflection and then looked away. Everyone else was wearing bright pastels and hot psychedelic colors, but she had put on a solid black leotard. A crow in a sea of tropical birds! she thought.

The music changed then, and the crowd suddenly shifted, following the lead of the instructor, who had leaped off the platform and was heading straight for Jen. Now what? Jen thought despairingly.

"Okay, everybody, in a circle!" she shouted. Darting to the center of the circle, she put her hands at her waist and began doing a series of rapid kicks, landing lightly on her feet each time. After about thirty seconds, she yelled cheerfully, "You're next!" and immediately left her spot in the center to tag one of the class. Jen was terrified that she was the intended victim, and breathed a sigh of relief when a thin girl next to her was tagged.

The girl dashed into the center of the circle,

launching into a complicated series of steps. She seemed to be smiling right at Jen the whole time, and Jen had the sinking feeling that her reprieve was only temporary. She *knew* she was going to be next, and she didn't have a clue what she would do. Struggling to keep up, she tried to remember some of the steps on Sally's Jane Fonda tape, but her mind was a blank. She couldn't remember a single thing!

She was wondering if she could feign a heart attack — or would someone try to revive her? — when the thin girl tapped her shoulder. Her worst nightmare was coming true — she was next! Grinning weakly, she scampered to the middle of the circle, her mind reeling. Everybody was jogging in place, clapping in time to the beat, waiting for her to do something . . . aerobic. She looked wildly around the circle for Lucy and Tracy, but couldn't spot them. The music was so loud, burning into her ears, and her arms and legs felt like lead. If ever there was a time for clear thought, this was it.

Think! Think! she ordered. Dimly, gradually, her mind began to function, but it was hopeless. Only one thought surfaced in her brain: I never should have had that muffin!

Chapter 12

"I can't believe it!" Jen said forty-five minutes later. "The Riveaus are gone again." She looked morosely around the mirrored aerobics room. The class had ended a few minutes earlier, and she and her friends had posted themselves by the doorway, watching as the last of the clients trailed out.

"If they were ever here," Lucy snorted. She leaned down and rubbed her aching calves. Her throat was parched, her chest was tight, and the backs of her legs felt like they were on fire. Who would ever think that an aerobics class could be so exhausting!

"I told you I saw them!" Tracy said furiously. She brushed a limp strand of blonde hair out of her eyes, and wished she had worn a ponytail. Her hair was ruined, she thought, glancing at herself in the mirror, and worse, her eye makeup was sliding right off her face. The dark blue eye shadow had been a giant mistake. Apparently it wasn't water-proof and now she had horrible rings under her eyes, just like the ghouls in *Night of the Living Dead*.

"Then where are they?" Lucy said calmly. She nodded her head toward the knot of people zipping up their gym bags and heading out the door. In a moment, the room would be empty.

"How should I know?" Tracy's eyes were blazing. "You were supposed to be watching the middle of the room — maybe you missed them. Or maybe Jen missed them," she said pointedly. "You both were so busy trying to keep up with the exercises, you weren't watching the floor."

"Hey, let's not start blaming each other." Jen's voice was low and firm. "There's another possibility, you know."

"What's that?" Lucy and Tracy said in unison.

"That the person wearing the Riveaus left early. It would be easy to slip out the door, especially if he — or she — was standing at the back of the room. Or maybe it happened when we all joined in a circle," she said thoughtfully.

Lucy was silent for a moment, and then looked at Tracy. "She's right," she said quietly. "I shouldn't have jumped on you like that."

"That's okay," Tracy said, mollified. The instructor picked up a pile of cassettes and started to switch off the lights. "Looks like this is it," Tracy added. "We've lost the trail again."

"Not necessarily," Lucy said briskly. "C'mon, gang, let's head for the water fountain and plan our next strategy."

Outside in the hall, they ran into Steve. He looked pale and tired and had a peculiar rolling walk.

"What happened?" Tracy said anxiously. "You didn't get hurt, did you?

"No, I'm fine," Steve rasped. "Except I never want to see another weight-lifting room again in my life. That Nordic tracking machine almost killed me."

"I've seen those," Jen said. "It's supposed to be great for your arms and legs," she explained to Tracy. "You feel just like you're skiing."

"Right," Steve said, groaning as he leaned down to get a drink. "You feel like you're skiing down Mount Everest." He gave a weak smile, and straightened up gingerly. "I think I overdid it a little. Would you guys mind very much if I just sat out the next few minutes?"

"Of course not," Lucy assured him. "Why don't you relax in the lounge until you get your second wind? You're worth more to us alive than dead," she joked.

"I could stay with him," Tracy volunteered. "We could sit on the sofa over there," she said, pointing to a large white sectional, "and order some drinks from the juice bar. Steve is probably dehydrated from all that exercise," she said.

"C'mon, Florence Nightingale," Lucy said, dragging Tracy by the arm. "Steve will be fine by himself for a little while. We need you with us."

"Oh, all right," Tracy muttered, annoyed. "What are we doing now?" She had already ruined her looks for this project — what more could they possibly want from her?

"The three of us," Lucy said firmly, "are going to pay a visit to the sauna, the steam room, and the whirlpool."

"The steam room?" Tracy wailed. "You've got to be kidding! It's so . . . wet in there."

"But it's good for you," Jen explained. "The humidity. . . ."

"Don't talk to me about humidity," Tracy said. "If I even get close to a drop of rain, my hair frizzes hopelessly."

Lucy and Jen exchanged a look. Here they were at a crucial stage in their investigation, and Tracy was pulling her prom-queen act!

"So cover it with a towel," Lucy said, unimpressed. She steered her friends down another long corridor with a row of lockers. "We have to strip off our leotards here," she explained. "You can either put your stuff in the lockers, or just pile it along the wall. No one bothers it."

"Strip off our leotards?" Tracy said, horrified. Her hands instinctively clutched her royal blue Spandex leotard as though Lucy was going to make a grab for it. "But what do we wear — in there?" she asked, pointing to a heavy glass door.

"A towel, of course," Lucy said. She picked up a large, snowy white towel from a pile and tossed one to Tracy. "On second thought, take two," she added mischievously, "since you're so concerned about your hair."

A few minutes later, Tracy sat on a white-tiled ledge, enveloped in clouds of steam. It was so humid! She had tried to protect her hair by wrapping it in a turban, but she could feel the terrible moist heat seep right through, turning it into limp spaghetti. If this was what detective work was like, she never wanted to get involved again! She'd foolishly thought it would be fun, maybe even interesting, and definitely a way to meet cute guys. But look what had happened! Here she was, hot and clammy on a tile ledge like some stupid tropical plant!

"How's it going?" Jen said, sitting down next to her.

"I think my toenails are melting," Tracy answered. "Any second now, I'm just going to fade away. You'll see a little puddle of wax on the floor, just like in *The Wizard of Oz*." She paused dramatically and took a deep breath. "Not that you and Lucy care." Her lower lip trembled and Jen wondered if she was going to cry.

Jen hesitated. When Tracy was in one of these moods, sometimes it was better to just let her talk it out and enjoy feeling sorry for herself. "I don't think it's as bad as all that," she said gently.

"Hah!" Tracy turned to glare at her. "Easy for you to say." She tucked her chin down dejectedly on her chest, staring at the wet floor. The heat was rising around her in clouds — it was like sitting over a steam grate!

"Well, you can't blame Lucy," Jen said quietly. "It's going to take all three of us to look around in here. It's so darn steamy!" She glanced at the row of women sitting on an identical ledge across from them. Their faces were somewhat clouded by the mist, but she could see that they could be clones. All three were tall, skinny and had white towels wrapped around their bodies and heads. Two of them had their eyes closed, and the third one looked like she was meditating — she was sitting cross-legged in a yoga position, with her hands resting on her knees. How in the world was she going to strike up a conversation with them? She had to get them to say something — anything — just to see if they had a Southern accent.

"Will you be okay for a few minutes?" she whispered to Tracy. "I want to check out those women across the way."

Tracy stared at her. "Of course I'll be all right," she said with surprise. "It's not like I'm *going* anywhere. How could I, dressed like this?" she added, glancing down at the soaking towel wrapped around her.

Jen stood up quickly, before Tracy could launch into another litany of complaints. "Okay, just wait here, and keep your eyes and ears open," she pleaded. "Remember — the main thing we're looking for is a Southern accent!"

"Yeah, sure," Tracy muttered. The moment Jen moved into the swirling mists, Tracy leaned her head back against the slippery tile wall. She had no intention of stumbling around this . . . hothouse . . . on a crazy errand, looking for a robber who probably didn't even exist.

She yawned then, wondering why the heat was making her so drowsy, and pictured a wonderful scene between herself and Steve. This stupid "investigation," as Jen called it, was finally over, and her hair and makeup were back to their usual state of perfection. Suddenly a voice broke into her dream.

"Tracy, Tracy, wake up!" Dimly, Tracy opened her eyes to see Lucy bending over her. She glanced down at her hand and saw that Lucy had been twisting her fingers.

"Darn it, that hurts!" Tracy said groggily. She yanked her hand away from Lucy and gently rubbed her sore fingers. "What's wrong with you?"

"I couldn't wake you up," Lucy hissed. "I thought maybe you had passed out in here." She peered closely at Tracy and then pulled her to her feet. "You don't look too good," she said. "I think we need to get you out of here right away. Jen's already outside waiting for us."

Tracy stumbled obediently after Lucy, lurching to the door. She was in a funny, dreamlike state, almost like sleep-walking, she decided.

"How's she doing?" Jen's voice was anxious.

"I think she was in there too long," Lucy said, propping Tracy against the wall while she considered their next move. "But don't you worry, Tracy. We'll have you fixed up in a jiffy," she said solicitously. "The first thing we'll do is take this silly towel off your hair."

"Ah, that's much better," Tracy said gratefully. She immediately felt about twenty degrees cooler, and for once she didn't even care about her hair.

"Then we'll move right along to the next step."

"The next step?" Tracy asked.

"First we cool down and take a short break. Then you and I are heading for the whirlpool," Lucy said. "Jen will check out the sauna."

"You mean there's more?" Tracy faltered. "I thought this was it. I thought we were going home now."

Lucy shrugged. "We can't give up now, Tracy. I've got the feeling we're getting closer to those Riveaus every minute."

"The only thing I'm getting closer to is death," Tracy moaned. She started to sink slowly to the floor, but Lucy grabbed her, and flung an arm around her waist.

"Tracy, please! You'll feel much better after we cool off and then, it's into the whirlpool!" Tracy was offering passive resistance, letting her body go limp. What could she say to convince her? "Uh, Tracy," she began, "you know how you always admired those millionaires on *Lifestyles of the Rich and Famous*?"

"Of course. *Lifestyles* is my favorite show!" Tracy opened one eye cautiously.

Lucy nodded encouragingly. "Well, you're finally going to get a chance to live like one of those jet-setters," she promised.

"How?" Tracy's voice was weak, but suspicious.

"You know how the movie stars are always sitting around in Jacuzzis?"

"Sure. They even have lunch served in their Jacuzzi."

Lucy laughed. "Well, I've got a big surprise for you. I'm taking you to a Jacuzzi right now. It's the chance of a lifetime," she said in a wheedling tone.

"A Jacuzzi? You said we were going to the

whirlpool." Tracy started to slump back toward the floor again.

"Did I?" Lucy said wildly. "Well, I meant Jacuzzi. C'mon, you'll see!" Before Tracy could think of anything else to say, Lucy dragged her back to the lockers where they had stashed their tank suits. The whirlpool was their last hope, she thought, discouraged. That is, if Jen didn't find anything in the sauna.

Meanwhile, Jen, still in a towel, had just made the discovery of her life. She was perched on a bench, preparing to face the sauna, when she tripped over a pair of shoes stashed against the wall. She wearily kicked them out of her way and then did a double take.

They were Riveaus.

And not just any Riveaus, but gray and black with suede trim. They were *the* Riveaus. Her immediate reaction was one of elation, followed by sheer panic. She was alone, with no backup. Steve was miles away in the lounge, and Tracy and Lucy were probably getting changed into swimsuits for the whirlpool. Darn! she thought. What should I do?

She didn't dare take a chance and run to get Steve or the girls — with her luck, the owner of the Riveaus would take that moment to appear, grab her shoes, and disappear out of their lives forever. So that left . . . what?

Her heart was hammering in her chest, and she forced herself to take a deep breath and try to think the situation through logically. One of her favorite TV characters was Mr. Spock on *Star Trek*, and she tried to think of how her hero would approach the problem. He would be cool and analytical, she decided. And unemotional. Yes, that was what she must aim for.

She closed her eyes for a second and ran through the possibilities. There was no reason to panic. The Riveaus weren't going anywhere — and if necessary, she could outwait the owner. The thought made her feel a lot better and she decided she'd better plan her encounter with the owner of the shoes. What would she say to her? Would she —

"Ohmigosh!" she said out loud. "It's a woman." Of course! Only women used this sauna, so that solved one problem right there. Now all she had to do was —

She jumped as the Riveaus suddenly began moving away from her — they were sliding right out from under her feet! Her eyes flew open just in time to see a tall redhead flash an apologetic smile. Was she finally face-to-face with the robber? If the girl had a Southern accent. . . .

"Gee, I didn't mean to wake you up," the girl said. "But, like, I need my shoes, you know?" She grinned. "Sure hot in here, isn't it?"

"Sure is," Jen agreed, her spirits sinking.

The girl had an accent all right. And Jen recognized the accent immediately. After all, she had seen all those *Rocky* movies. The woman wasn't Southern at all — she sounded just like Sylvester Stallone!

Chapter 13

"I'm not sure I understand any of this," Susan Hillard was saying in her whiny voice the following Monday. The group had assembled for an emergency meeting in the Cedar Groves cafeteria at lunchtime, and Lucy was trying patiently to explain why all their leads had fallen through.

"What don't you get?" Nora asked tightly. They hadn't heard a word from Susan since she had walked out of the strategy meeting at Jen's house. She had made it clear that night that she didn't want to be part of the group, but she still couldn't resist making fun of their efforts. Typical, Nora thought, annoyed.

"Well," Susan said, inspecting one of her fingernails, "are you absolutely sure that this woman in the health club wasn't involved in the robbery?"

"I'm positive," Jen told her firmly.

"But she had the right shoes," Tracy pointed out. "And the right color hair. You said so yourself." She looked down the table at Steve Crowley, hoping he would agree with her, but he seemed lost in thought.

"But definitely not the right accent, or the right voice," Jen insisted. "I know what I heard! That woman has never been south of Philadelphia."

Everyone was silent for a moment, and then Tommy Ryder said, "I can't believe the robbers just vanished into thin air. That never happens on television," he offered thoughtfully.

"Well it does in real life," Lucy said wryly. "Unless you have some ideas we may have missed."

"Hah — that will be the day!" Tommy's sidekick, Mitch Pauley hooted.

Tommy pretended to pour his chocolate milk over his friend's head, and Susan Hillard nudged him sharply in the ribs.

"If you've got an idea, let's hear it," she grumbled.

"Well," Tommy said slowly, settling back in his seat, "the way I see it is this. The robbers are hiding out somewhere, and there's a really good chance we're not ever going to find them."

"Right," Jen agreed.

"Okay," Tommy said, swatting away Mitch Pauley who had retaliated by stealing a brownie off his tray. "Now . . . that means the crime is going to be committed whether we like it or not."

"Right again, Sherlock," Susan said sarcastically.

"So . . . there's only one thing left to do." He paused dramatically. "Someone should go to the bank and warn the manager that they're going to be robbed."

"Oh, sure!" Mitch sneered. "That makes a lot of sense!"

"Wait a minute, it's not such a bad idea," Steve spoke up. "I didn't say anything about it that day I was at the bank with Tracy, but the same idea occurred to me." He leaned his elbows on the table and looked thoughtfully at Lucy. "You said you're pretty sure that Captain Simpson at the police station isn't going to do anything about it."

"I'm *sure* he isn't!" Nora exclaimed. "He thinks we imagined the whole thing."

"Then I think Tommy's right," Steve said flatly. "If we can't prevent the crime from happening, the least we can do is try to warn the intended victim. In this case, it's the bank."

"You're absolutely right." Nora looked around the table and saw that most of the group was nodding in agreement. "When do you want to go?"

"I think we should go today," Steve said.

"We? You mean all of us? It's going to look pretty funny for a bunch of kids to go trooping in there."

Steve shook his head. "No, I think just two of us should go."

"Two of us?" Tracy blurted out. "Do you mean you want me to go with you, Steve?"

Steve grinned. "Well, we were partners before, and we did okay. What do you say we try again?"

"I . . . yes!" Tracy said. She was going back to the bank with Steve. Fantastic. She was wondering if she would have time to comb her hair, when something hit her chair so hard from behind that her chin almost landed in her spaghetti!

"What in the — " she turned angrily to see Jason Anthony smiling down at her.

"Sorry about that," he said breathlessly. He bent down to inspect his skateboard. "Don't worry about it, it doesn't seem to be damaged."

"Damaged!" she sputtered. "I'm going to damage you! You . . . you . . . !"

"Hey, easy," Jason said, backing away. "It's not like they have brakes on these things, you know. Sometimes even with the best of skill, you . . . uh . . . collide with things. Anyway," he said, scooting quickly over to Lucy, "you're the one I came to see."

"My lucky day," Lucy sighed.

"It could be," Jason said, giving a devilish smile. His red hair was tousled and his oversized navy blue T-shirt was sticking out of his faded jeans. "I've got some information that you'd love to have."

"Jason, you don't have anything that I'd love to have."

He suddenly perched on the edge of the table, nearly landing in Susan's Jell-O. "Hey, watch it!" she yelled.

"Information about the Riveaus," he said quietly, watching Lucy's face.

"What?" Lucy was so excited she jumped to her feet. "What kind of information?" she demanded.

Jason rubbed his chin and stared at the ceiling, pretending to ponder the question. "What kind of information?" he said in his W. C. Fields voice. "Ah, that's hard to say, little lady. That's hard to say."

"Maybe this will help you spit it out," Tommy Ryder said, rushing around the table and grabbing Jason around the neck.

"I . . . I . . ." Jason gurgled helplessly.

"Let him go, Tommy," Jen pleaded. "He can't talk if you're going to choke him to death!"

"Then talk!" Tommy ordered. He released Jason, who fell against Susan. "Firsthand information," he rasped.

"You have firsthand information?" Nora said eagerly. "What does that mean?"

"That means," he said, drawing himself up to his full height of five foot six inches, "that I saw them." He waited for this to sink in, and then added, "But if you want to know where, it's going to cost you."

"Darn you, Jason Anthony!" Lucy was half out of her seat, but Steve beat her to it.

"If you've seen those Riveaus, it's your duty to tell us about it," Steve said. He towered menacingly over Jason, who jumped lightly to one side, just out of reach.

"What are you going to do, make a citizen's arrest?" Jason chortled.

"No, we're going to do something better,"

Lucy said calmly. She reached down and grabbed his battered skateboard. "We're going to take a hostage."

"Not my skateboard!" Jason wailed.

Lucy tucked the skateboard under her chair, and planted her foot on it. "Then talk," she said sweetly. "And no harm will come to your . . . friend."

"I — all right!" Jason agreed, throwing himself into an empty chair. His face was flushed and he brushed a lock of red hair out of his eyes. "You're probably not going to believe this," he began, "but I saw them right here at school."

Nora blinked. "You mean a kid's wearing the same kind of Riveaus the robber had — black and gray with suede trim?"

"Nope, I mean the robber's wearing them. A guy maybe in his thirties, dressed in jeans — expensive ones — and a tweed blazer." Jason folded his arms and sat back, enjoying being the center of attention. "And guess what — he's right upstairs in the front hall. The east wing."

"That's impossible," Lucy murmured.

"Impossible, but true," Jason said, reverting to his W. C. Fields voice. "Now can I have my skateboard back?"

For a moment, everyone was too stunned to reply, and then Nora said curtly, "What are we waiting for, gang? Lucy, give him his skateboard and let's get upstairs before the bell rings!"

Moments later, Nora and Lucy peeked nervously around the corner, hoping that Mrs. Carpenter, in the office, wouldn't see them. Steve and Tracy were posted with Jen at the opposite end of the hall, and the other kids were guarding the exit doors.

"I think we've covered everything," Lucy whispered. "If he's still in the building, you can be darn sure he's not going anywhere. We've got him!"

Nora nodded. She admired Lucy's optimism, but she couldn't shake the nagging feeling that he was going to get away again. If he really *was* the robber, she reminded herself. But everything seemed to fit, she thought, trying to fight down the little bubble of excitement building up inside her. She had to stay calm, she had to keep her wits about her, because any minute —

"There he is!" Lucy hissed in her ear. Nora's heart lurched as she followed Lucy's gaze to the teachers' lounge, right off the main hallway. A man was coming out . . . he was exactly like Jason had described, early thirties, good-looking, with black hair, and snapping dark eyes. He was dressed in a tailored tweed blazer with a white shirt that he wore open at the neck. And Jason was right about the jeans . . . they were tapered, designer ones.

And he was wearing Riveaus. Gray and black ones with suede trim.

"Ohmigosh," Nora blurted out. "Now what do we do?"

"We stop him," Lucy said, darting away from the side of the wall. "C'mon!"

Pulling Nora along with her, she began walking casually toward the man who was strolling along the corridor, looking idly at the football trophies in the glass display cases.

"He's probably looking for something else to steal," Nora whispered disapprovingly.

"Sshh," Lucy warned her. "Just act natural."

"What are we going to do?"

"I don't know," Lucy said, quickening her pace. "I'll have to think of something when we get up to him."

"That's reassuring," Nora sighed.

"Excuse me," Lucy said brightly. The man turned, and they were just a few feet away from him. Up close, Nora could see that he was really good-looking and looked vaguely famil-

158

iar. He had piercing dark eyes, a strong jaw, and perfect features. If Nora didn't know better, she would think he looked more like an actor or a model, than a bank robber.

"Yes? Can I help you?" Nora's heart nearly stopped — the man had a French accent!

"I . . . that is . . . we need a hall pass," Lucy stammered. "We need to go to the library, and we forgot to get one from our study hall teacher."

The man smiled, flashing a set of white, even teeth. "I would love to help you, but there is a problem." He put the accent on the second syllable. "I am not a teacher here."

"Oh, we're so sorry," Lucy said, "When I saw you coming out of the teachers' lounge, I thought you were one of the new substitutes they hired."

He shrugged, spreading his hands in front of him. "Unfortunately not."

Lucy waited. How could she get him to say the *real* reason he was there! Just as she was wondering what to say next, Mrs. Carpenter, the assistant principal, came over.

"Oh, there you are!" she said cheerily. "Mr. Donovan and the others are waiting for you in the office."

"Thank you madame." He gave a low bow.

Lucy gave Nora a disgusted look. Mrs. Carpenter wouldn't be so happy if she knew she was talking to a bank robber! And why was Mr. Donovan, the school principal, seeing him? She was wondering what to do next when Mrs. Carpenter gave her a sharp look.

"Shouldn't you girls be in class?"

"Oh, yes," Nora gulped, "we're on our way." She smiled and pulled Lucy along the corridor with her. "Now what?" she mouthed.

"Just keep walking until I tell you they're out of sight." They were almost at the end of the hall, when Lucy stopped and pretended to tie her shoe. "They're gone," she said, straightening up. "They must have gone into Mr. Donovan's office." She paused. "There's only one thing left to do, Nora," she said solemnly. "We have to go back there."

"What will we say?" Nora's mind was reeling. The robber — she was sure of it — was talking to Mr. Donovan right this minute! What was going on?

"You know what our drama coach always says," Lucy said. "Improvise!"

"I'm not sure this is the best way to handle it," Nora said a couple of minutes later. They were standing outside Mrs. Carpenter's glass-enclosed office next door to Mr. Donovan's.

Jen, Tracy, and Steve were right behind them, and unless she was mistaken, she heard Jason Anthony somewhere down the hall, careening toward them.

"Got a better idea?" Lucy asked.

"Uh, no, actually . . ." Nora hesitated.

"Then let's go!"

Lucy flung open the door, ignored Mrs. Carpenter's astonished look, and marched right into Mr. Donovan's office, with the rest of the group bringing up the rear.

"What is the meaning of this?" Mrs. Carpenter said, struggling to wade through the tight knot of bodies piling into the principal's office. "I didn't give them permission to come in, Mr. Donovan," she said.

"We gave ourselves permission!" Lucy's voice quivered a little as Mr. Donovan got up from his desk.

"What's going on here?" His voice was dangerously quiet.

"Looks like you've got a student revolt on your hands," someone said in a Dolly Parton voice. Lucy's eyes swung in the direction of the voice, and saw a slim, young, red-haired woman smiling at her. Of course! The girl from Temptations. Today she was wearing a pair of white jeans with a fringed cowboy shirt and tan leather boots. "It's not a revolt," Lucy said, taking a step backward and landing squarely on Nora's foot. Mr. Donovan looked furious, and she had to remind herself that she'd probably get a medal once the truth came out. "It's . . . it's . . ."

"Oh, they probably just want autographs," the redhead said good-naturedly. "Ever since that last Disney movie, I can't go anywhere without being recognized." She smiled and patted her flowing auburn hair as if she didn't mind a single bit.

"Autographs?" Nora said, puzzled. "You think we want autographs?"

"Or a part in our movie," the man with the French accent teased. "Everybody in America wants to be an actor!"

"A movie!" Tracy Douglas pushed her way through the crowd. "You're here to make a movie?"

"But of course." The Frenchman shrugged. "You did not tell the students?"

"Not yet," Mr. Donovan said, settling back at his desk. He looked uncomfortable for a moment, capping and uncapping his fountain pen. Then he came to a decision. "Well, kids," he said briskly, "since you've already blown their cover, you might as well hear the whole story.

These people are from Nova Studios in Montreal."

Nova Studios! Tracy thought excitedly. She had just rented a video produced by Nova the week before!

"This is Mr. Pierre Phillippe, who will be producing a movie right here in Cedar Groves, and Miss Shawna Stevens, who has the starring role."

"Pierre Phillippe," Nora blurted out. "Didn't you used to be an actor? I think I saw you as 'Claude' on *The Promise of Tomorrow*."

Pierre Phillippe smiled. "I was on the show for two years," he said proudly.

"Wow — a real live actor," Tracy murmured.

"No, now I'm a real live director," he said solemnly and Shawna Stevens laughed.

"But what are you doing here?" Steve Crowley asked. "How come you're not making the movie in Hollywood or New York?"

"Good question," Pierre complimented him. "The truth is, we did scout some locations in Beverly Hills, but nothing looked right. We finally decided that the best way to give a — how do you say — small-town flavor to the film, was to go to a small town!"

"We tried to keep this as quiet as possible,"

Mr. Donovan went on, "but I guess I should have realized that word would get out anyway."

"It always does," Shawna said. "Pierre, remember that waitress in Temptations? We had to make her promise not to talk about the movie. She was so excited she was going to tell the whole town!"

"So that *was* you in Temptations that day?" Nora spoke up.

"Probably." She shrugged. "I'm a nut about ice cream. Hey, did you see us in there? You should have come over to introduce yourselves."

"I wish we had," Lucy said. It would have saved a lot of trouble, she added silently.

"Well, now that you know about the movie, how about if you all go back to your classes, and I'll keep you posted?" Mr. Donovan suggested. "As soon as the details are finalized, there will be a general assembly. I know there's going to be a lot of interest in the production."

Interest? Nora thought. That has to be the understatement of the year!

"So you're really not criminals," Tracy piped up. "And you're really not here to rob a bank," she said innocently.

"Only on film," Pierre said in a surprised

tone. "But how did you know the movie was about the bank robbery?"

"Just a lucky guess," Tracy said, giving him her brightest smile. She wondered if she could audition for him. Maybe she could even be discovered! "But how come you're here at school? Are you going to use some of the kids as extras?"

"We'll definitely use quite a few of you," Pierre Phillippe said graciously. "I'm sure there's a lot of talent here."

"And guess what?" Shawna said. "They're casting a cat in a leading role. Isn't that the cutest thing you've ever heard? Now, I can't give away the plot," she said coyly, "but this cat has a lot to do with the bank robbery."

"All right, time to go back to class," Mrs. Carpenter broke in. She had finally maneuvered her way to the front of the room, and was preparing to herd them back to the hall. "C'mon, kids, you've interrupted this meeting long enough."

"Just a second," Jen pleaded, as she was being swept out the door. "What's the name of the movie?"

"*The Great Cat Caper*," she heard Shawna say, before she was propelled backward toward the hall.

They trooped into the hall just as the bell rang. Most of the kids went scurrying to their next class, but Lucy, Tracy, and Jen clustered around Nora.

"I can't believe it," Nora said, dazed. "There's not going to be a bank robbery after all. What we heard them talking about in Temptations was a *movie*."

"*The Great Cat Caper*." Jen was excited. "Don't you love the title? And just think — they're going to choose a cat right here in Cedar Groves to be the star. Murphy would be perfect! He's got gray and white stripes and I know he'd be adorable on camera. I'll call his new owners today and see if he can audition."

"A movie!" Lucy laughed. "Who would ever believe it!"

"I believe it," Tracy said dreamily. She clutched her notebook to her chest and did a little dance step. "And it's more than a movie."

"More than a movie?" Steve came up quietly behind them, and linked arms with Jen.

"Of course," she nodded happily. She was so busy planning what she would wear to audition, she barely noticed him. "It's much, much more. It's the biggest thing to ever happen to me! It's the chance of a lifetime." She took out her mirror and decided to touch up her lip gloss then and there. If there were going to be movie producers at the school from now on, she'd have to look her best every single minute!

Lucy and Nora exchanged a look and started down the hall just as the second bell rang. Tracy was still standing in the middle of the corridor with a dreamy expression on her face, and Jen and Steve were looking at each other as if they had more on their minds than the movie.

"Well, at least that's that," Lucy said wearily. She fumbled in her notebook for her French homework, and was relieved when she found it. She rapidly went over her afternoon schedule. French Composition, English Lit, an Honor Society meeting, and then her day would be over.

"What do you mean?" Nora was giving her a funny look.

"I mean . . . the mystery is over. We don't have to worry anymore. There's not going to be any bank robbery, and things can finally get back to normal around here."

"Back to normal?" Nora laughed. "Lucy, are you kidding? In case you haven't noticed, things are never normal around here."

There's nothing like a mall — especially with the Cedar Groves Junior High eighth grade in charge! Read Junior High #15, **THE NIGHT THE EIGHTH GRADE RAN THE MALL.**

SUNFIRE®

**Read all about the fascinating young women who lived
and loved during America's most turbulent times!**

☐ 32774-7		**AMANDA** Candice F. Ransom	**$2.95**
☐ 33064-0		**SUSANNAH** Candice F. Ransom	**$2.95**
☐ 33156-6		**DANIELLE** Vivian Schurfranz	**$2.95**
☐ 33241-4	#5	**JOANNA** Jane Claypool Miner	**$2.95**
☐ 33242-2	#6	**JESSICA** Mary Francis Shura	**$2.95**
☐ 33239-2	#7	**CAROLINE** Willo Davis Roberts	**$2.95**
☐ 33688-6	#14	**CASSIE** Vivian Schurfranz	**$2.95**
☐ 33686-X	#15	**ROXANNE** Jane Claypool Miner	**$2.95**
☐ 41468-2	#16	**MEGAN** Vivian Schurfranz	**$2.75**
☐ 41438-0	#17	**SABRINA** Candice F. Ransom	**$2.75**
☐ 42134-4	#18	**VERONICA** Jane Claypool Miner	**$2.75**
☐ 40049-5	#19	**NICOLE** Candice F. Ransom	**$2.25**
☐ 42228-6	#20	**JULIE** Vivian Schurfranz	**$2.75**
☐ 40394-X	#21	**RACHEL** Vivian Schurfranz	**$2.50**
☐ 40395-8	#22	**COREY** Jane Claypool Miner	**$2.50**
☐ 40717-1	#23	**HEATHER** Vivian Schurfranz	**$2.50**
☐ 40716-3	#24	**GABRIELLE** Mary Francis Shura	**$2.50**
☐ 41000-8	#25	**MERRIE** Vivian Schurfranz	**$2.75**
☐ 41012-1	#26	**NORA** Jeffie Ross Gordon	**$2.75**
☐ 41191-8	#27	**MARGARET** Jane Claypool Miner	**$2.75**
☐ 41207-8	#28	**JOSIE** Vivian Schurfranz	**$2.75**
☐ 41416-X	#29	**DIANA** Mary Francis Shura	**$2.75**
☐ 42043-7	#30	**RENÉE** Vivian Schurfranz (February '89)	**$2.75**

Scholastic Inc., P.O. Box 7502, 2932 East McCarty Street, Jefferson City, MO 65102

Please send me the books I have checked above. I am enclosing $ _____
(please add $1.00 to cover shipping and handling). Send check or money-order–no cash or
C.O.D.'s please.

Name _____

Address _____

City _____ State/Zip _____

Please allow four to six weeks for delivery. Offer good in U.S.A. only. Sorry, mail order not available
to residents of Canada. Prices subject to change.

SUN 888

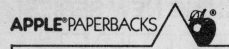